First hog-feeding adventure

The big pig wasn't budging. It was too busy stuffing its fat belly.

She gathered her skirt and pulled gently, h— se it out. When that didn'— ain. "Get—off—my—gow—

She gave a final ya— the same time the sow deci—

With the weight sud— fell back into the muck. Th— she felt herself sinking into the wet, slimy earth.

"Aauughh!" she howled and then opened her eyes to survey the mess. Before she could take stock, she heard something.

Laughter.

She looked around the paddocks and barns. Her gaze slid by then came back to rest on the figure perched not fifteen feet away on the fence. Clay was clutching his stomach with uncontained mirth.

Anger boiled inside her. She struggled to stand up and realized her skirts had risen to her knees revealing her frilled bloomers beneath them. "Aauughh!" she howled again and flung the sodden skirts back down around her ankles before trying to stand again.

Clay continued to display unbridled mirth.

"Of all the"—her hand slipped in the mud—"nerve!" She turned over on her knees, knowing she would ruin her gown but not caring anymore. "Instead of standing there laughing like a"—she pushed to her feet, aware that her backside was sticking up in the air—"a complete nincompoop!"

"Hold on there, Fancy Pants, and I'll—"

She sucked in a breath of foul air. "Well!" She rose to her full height, albeit unsteadily. "You, Sir, are no gentleman! How dare you mention my—my—unmentionables!"

"No offense, Ma'am. I've never seen such fancy duds—"

"Will you stop speaking of them!"

DENISE HUNTER lives in Indiana with her husband and three active young sons. As the only female of the household, every day is a new adventure, but Denise holds on to the belief that her most important responsibility in this life is to raise her children in such a way that they will love and fear the Lord. The message Denise wants her writing to convey is that "God needs to be the center of our lives. If He isn't, everything else is out of kilter."

HEARTSONG PRESENTS

Books by Denise Hunter
HP328—Stranger's Bride
HP379—Never a Bride

Don't miss out on any of our super romances. Write to us at the following address for information on our newest releases and club information.

Heartsong Presents Readers' Service
PO Box 719
Uhrichsville, OH 44683

Or visit us at www.heartsongpresents.com

Bittersweet Bride

Denise Hunter

Heartsong Presents

A note from the author:
*I love to hear from my readers! You may correspond with me
by writing:*   **Denise Hunter**
                            Author Relations
                            PO Box 719
                            Uhrichsville, OH 44683

ISBN 1-58660-526-7

BITTERSWEET BRIDE

All Scripture quotations are taken from the King James Version of
the Bible.

All of the characters and events in this book are fictitious. Any
resemblance to actual persons, living or dead, or to actual events
is purely coincidental.

Cover illustration by Lorraine Bush.

PRINTED IN THE U.S.A.

one

Mara Lawton's tiny feet drew to a halt the moment she saw him. Her hands, in their vain attempt to smooth her already perfect gown, fell forgotten to her side. Her breath caught and held, but her heart seemed to keep tempo with the fiddle music pouring through the barn doors.

He stood surrounded by men, his foot propped on a bale of hay, watching the couples swirl in the stale night air. The lantern light flickered, and dark shadows shifted on the harsh planes of his cheekbones. She was suddenly very glad she'd turned down two suitors, opting to attend unescorted.

"Stand up straight, Mara—you're slouching." Her mother fussed with Mara's hair as she pulled back her shoulders, drawing her torso erect.

"Go on in, Princess." Her father guided her through the door with a hand on her waist.

Her gaze hadn't shifted from the newcomer, and she noted the broad set of his shoulders, the way he stood a head above the men around him. *My, my, my.*

She drew as deep a breath as her corset allowed and attempted to regulate her breathing. The air, still pungent with the odor of manure and musty hay, filled her lungs.

"Howdy, Mara."

She pulled her gaze from the man to see Daniel Parnell shifting at her side, his fingers crumpling the brim of his hat.

She offered him a smile and a brief nod. "Daniel."

A smile wobbled on his face. "I—I hope you'll save me a dance."

She pulled a fan from her reticule and fluttered it before her face. "Certainly."

5

After offering to get her a drink, Daniel scurried off to the refreshment table.

Mara's gaze instantly sought the other man, but the spot in which he'd stood was empty. She glanced casually around the packed barn, and by the time Daniel returned with a drink in hand, she had found him once again.

Two hours later, with feet that ached from dancing, she stepped into the arms of Thomas More, taking care to keep a proper distance between them. The strains of "Lorena" floated through the building and up to the lofted beams of the ceiling. Mara exchanged pleasantries with her partner while keeping an eye on the man she'd found out was named Clay Stedman. She also knew he was Martha Stedman's nephew and had come to help with the ranch. It never failed to amaze her how much information one could glean from eager suitors. Clay had moved around the room throughout the night, talking with various men. He had danced with no one, though.

Not even her.

She tilted her chin and tossed a practiced smile at her dance partner. When she again glanced in Clay's direction, he was talking with Will Mathews, but his gaze was fixed on her. Her step faltered, but she quickly recovered and turned back to her partner with a coy smile that was more for Clay's benefit than Thomas's. Mara saw her partner's eyes light at the attention she bestowed on him, but the whole core of her being was focused on a man fifteen feet away.

Thomas whirled her again, and Clay was once again in her sights. She cast a casual glance toward him, delighted to find his attention still on her. This time she allowed her gaze to linger a moment, tilting her head and effecting a demure smile. The dance steps turned her away from Clay before she could see how he responded.

With a slow downward stroke of a bow, the tune ended, and she slipped from Thomas's arms, thanking him for the dance. Surely Clay would ask her to dance now. She'd danced with every other available man tonight.

Mara strolled to the refreshment table, a move that had her walking past Clay and Will. Her straight posture and dainty steps came naturally, as did the casual toss of her head that sent her blond curls dancing. As she approached the table, she noted the music had started again, a waltz.

"Hello, Jane," Mara said to the tall, skinny woman serving punch.

"Would you care for a drink?" Jane's face flushed an unbecoming shade of red, and the scar she had received from a riding accident remained ghostly white.

"Yes, please."

A tap on her shoulder sent her pulse hammering. *Finally he's asking me to dance.* She turned, her lips tilting in a welcome smile. "I don't believe we've—oh, it's you, Edward." The muscles in her face relaxed.

"Care to dance, Mara?"

"Perhaps later, Edward—I'm terribly parched." Only a few numbers were left, surely, and she had yet to dance with the one who had captured her attention. She gave Edward a dismissing smile, but he intercepted the punch from Jane and placed it in Mara's hand.

"Here you go," he said.

She took a sip and scanned the room for Clay. The room had thinned as people left the social and made their way home. Once again Clay was nowhere to be seen. Soon the musicians would announce the last song, and she hadn't even been introduced to the man. *Patience, Mara. He'll be around awhile if he's working the Stedmans' ranch.*

"There you are, Darling." Her mother appeared at her side with Doc Hathaway. Instantly Mara knew she was about to be pressured into dancing with her mother's latest marriage prospect for her. She suppressed a shudder.

"I was just telling Doctor Hathaway what an accomplished pianist you are, Dear."

Mara forced a smile to her lips. "Good evening, Doctor."

"Please, call me Morton." His smile crinkled the skin around his eyes, making her more aware of his advanced age.

The musicians announced their last tune, and she nearly groaned, knowing her mother would take full advantage of the opportunity.

"Well, there you've heard it. Why don't the two of you take a spin while I look for your father and William." She hurried off toward Mara's brother before either could respond.

"How about it, Mara? May I have the pleasure?"

Smothering her disappointment at the evening's ending, she acquiesced.

Later that night as Mara lay in her feather bed, she devised a plan. Clay Stedman was the most intriguing man to step foot in Cedar Springs in years, and she wasn't about to let him get away. As she drifted off to sleep she wondered if his hair was truly coal-black or if the dimness of the lanterns only made it seem that way.

Mara rose the next morning feeling unusually chipper. A new man was in town—a handsome, strong, magnetic man— and she intended to have him. If not forever, at least for a little while. All the appealing men in Cedar Springs were spoken for, and she had too easily captured the interest of the others. She had become bored with Edward and Thomas and the wrinkly, saggy Doctor Hathaway. Some fresh, new suitor was just what she craved.

Disappointment momentarily drained her spirits when she remembered that Clay had not asked her to dance the night before. *All the better,* she assured herself. A challenge was just what she needed to chase away the boredom. One could only practice piano and read *Harper's Bazaar* for so many hours of the day. She needed another pursuit, a diversion, and Clay Stedman was just the thing.

Later that afternoon Sadie pulled up the sides of Mara's hair and secured it with a pin. Mara put on her finest hat. She must look her best. The tangy scent of apple pie hung in the air. She would take it to him while it was still warm from the oven. She was just being a good neighbor after all. No need to tell him

Sadie had made it. What choice did Mara have? Sadie made the tastiest pies ever, and, besides, Mara couldn't even boil an egg. Clay needn't know that though. She would arrive on his doorstep with the pie, wearing her loveliest gown and her new French perfume, and the man would be after her like a bear after honey.

☙

Clay Stedman scooped up his eight-year-old sister, Beth, and settled on the small sofa while his aunt Martha cleaned up the supper dishes.

"What'd you do today, Squirt?"

"Aunt Martha showed me pictures of Uncle Edward. He had a beard this long!" She gestured to a line even with her shoulders. "And it was as white as Saint Nick's."

Clay laughed. "That he did."

"Aunt Martha said she's leaving on her trip soon. Can I stay by myself while you work?"

"Not a chance, Beth. You're not—"

"I could do it! I can cook and get dressed by myself and clean—"

Clay held up a hand to stop his sister's argument. "Now that's enough. I told you before we ever came here that we'd have to find someone to stay with you while Aunt Martha's gone, and nothing's changed."

Beth pouted, her full pink lip sticking out in dramatic fashion. Clay wondered if his aunt had found anyone to stay with Beth. With the grief of losing her husband three weeks before, he doubted she'd had any time or energy to search for temporary help while she visited her children back East.

Clay mussed Beth's hair and then stood up, tossing her the doll that sat beside him on the sofa. The little girl started a dialogue with her doll, Taffy, and he ambled off to the kitchen to find his aunt.

He found her in front of the sink, dabbing her eyes with the corner of her apron. He was about to slip away, not wanting to intrude on a private moment, but she spoke before he could leave.

"It's all right, Clay. You can come in."

He shifted his feet on the threshold. His aunt had always seemed to have eyes in the back of her head. Maybe it came with being a mother.

She began scrubbing a pan, and he stepped further into the room, not knowing what to say.

"I just miss him so. It seems so empty here without him."

Clay watched her blink back more tears. "It'll be good for you to visit with Margaret and Philip—and see those grandbabies."

She smiled faintly. "I'm hankering for them—that's true enough. But I leave next week, and I still haven't found anyone to take my place here. Someone who's used to cooking for a large crew and good with children. You'd think it wouldn't be so hard. Some of the church ladies have offered to lend a hand when they can, but we really need someone who can stay the whole two months. I can't bear the thought of Beth's being shuffled from one woman to the next. More than ever she needs a woman to attach to."

"She's got that with you."

Aunt Martha's face crinkled up, her lips trembling. "And I feel guilty leaving her—"

Clay took her in his arms. "Don't you worry—she'll be all right."

"She's still missing her mama." Aunt Martha's voice quivered. "Her daddy too, but she's got you at least. "

Clay patted her shoulder, wishing he knew what to say.

"This past week I've grown close to her, and now I'm leaving. She'll be so confused—"

His mind churned for a way to take the pressure off his overburdened aunt. Finally an idea came. "I'll find someone to take over for you, all right? You just pack your bags, and don't worry about a thing."

"But you don't know anyone—"

He gave her a hug. "Now when's the last time I failed to do what I set my mind to?"

She laughed and wiped her face with her apron. "You're as

stubborn as your daddy was."

He pretended to frown. "I'd as soon call it determined," he said, his eyes twinkling.

She laughed then picked up the pan again. "I've already asked most of the ladies in church. I don't know who you're going to find."

"You let me worry about that." He could always ask his workers for ideas. He had started back to the sitting room when his aunt stopped him.

"Clay—"

He turned.

"I don't know how to thank you for taking over here. I know you left a good job."

"Glad to do it, Aunt Martha. Don't give it another thought."

He slipped from the kitchen and into the sitting room and was surprised to find Beth gone. He sat down on the sofa again. He had left a good job—that was true enough. But the Stedman spread had plenty to offer. Here Beth had a chance to get away from the memories of Ma and Pa and start over. It gave him a chance to start over too. Nothing was left for him in Texas now anyway, and there hadn't been for some time. With his ma and pa gone, and his relationship with Victoria over—

Clay picked up the newspaper and snapped it open. Victoria. Even after all these months, the name rang through his head with all the bitterness of vinegar.

With new resolve he put the whole fiasco in the back of his mind. He had left Austin and Victoria and all her treachery behind. He wasn't going to let thoughts of her ruin this fresh start at his uncle's ranch.

He knew why he was thinking of her for the first time in weeks. It was that Lawton girl. He saw her the moment she entered the barn the night before. He couldn't miss her. She stood out like fireworks against a midnight sky, with her frilly emerald-green dress and golden curls. He thought of Victoria right off. Even more so after he saw her dancing and trifling with every male within a mile radius. No way he was going to get in that line. No siree. He'd had enough of spoiled debutantes.

No sooner had he started reading the first column when he heard a wagon approaching. Crossing the room in long strides, Clay reached the door in time to meet the knock.

two

Mara straightened her hat with her free hand while balancing the apple pie with the other. Sadie had laid a beautiful lattice crust on the pie and baked it to golden perfection, and Mara knew from past experience the taste would be as impressive as the appearance. She hadn't a clue how the woman turned out one masterpiece after another.

She approached the Stedmans' two-story clapboard home, her heart double-timing her footsteps. Would his eyes light up when he saw her? Maybe he would even invite her in for a slice of the pie. Oh, she hoped Martha Stedman wouldn't answer the door. That would ruin everything!

Mara pressed her lips together to give them color then bit them for good measure. She knew the ice-blue satin of her gown brought out her eyes and made the most of her creamy, flawless skin. Her mother said so every time she donned it, and the mirror didn't lie, after all.

Clearing her throat, she tapped lightly on the door. Her skin warmed with the flush of anticipation. She didn't know what she would say when he appeared, but she needn't worry. Words always found a way to her lips at the right moment.

Footfalls sounded behind the door, and she unconsciously checked her posture. The door creaked open, and she found herself staring into Clay's startled gray-brown eyes. Up close he was even more handsome. His disheveled black hair gave him a roguish look that left her breathless.

"Good evening, Mr. Stedman. I'm Mara Lawton." She held out her gloved hand, and he enveloped it with a strong grip. She saw a flash of admiration in his eyes and felt a twinge of satisfaction.

He nodded. "Miss Lawton."

"I've brought you a little welcoming gift, since we're practically neighbors." She pulled back the cheesecloth and presented him with the pie.

He blinked and pulled his gaze from hers to the offering in her hand, seeming to recover his wits. "Thanks, I—it looks good."

In his hands the pie suddenly looked half its original size.

"My, my," Mara said. "Does Texas breed all her men as tall and brawny as you?" The lilt in her voice was perfection itself. She completed the effect with a saucy smile.

His chin tipped back, and he narrowed his eyes. "I reckon my pa had more to do with that than geography." She noted his coolness and attempted a charming laugh. "Touché, Mr. Stedman." She batted her lashes effectively. "One's ancestors truly are the source of one's attributes."

He nodded. "Well, thanks for the—"

"I've most certainly acquired a trait or two from royalty myself. My family is directly descended from Queen Elizabeth the First, you know." Mara tilted her lips in a grin. He would surely be impressed by that.

His lips tightened. "Well, again, thanks for the—"

A little girl suddenly appeared at his side. "Aunt Martha said. . ."

Mara lost the rest of the words as she watched the girl wrap her arms around Clay. She had his shiny black hair, and her eyes were a deep sable-brown. Disappointment coiled in the pit of her stomach as she realized this must be his daughter. The black hair, the dark skin, the narrow nose. Anyone could see the resemblance.

"Please," the little girl pleaded.

"Mind your manners, Beth." His gaze met Mara's once again. "Miss Lawton, this is Beth. Beth, this is Miss Lawton."

"How do you do, Ma'am?"

"Beth." Mara nodded as she recovered. He was married! No wonder he hadn't asked her to dance. No wonder her suitors had been so free with information at the dance. He was no competitor of theirs if he was married.

"I reckon it's all right," Clay told the girl. "But you be back by nightfall."

"I will."

Mara moved aside as Beth scurried past her through the door.

Mara realized how foolish she must appear to Clay. Making eyes at him at the dance, bringing him a pie, flirting boldly with him on his own doorstep. Suddenly Mara was eager to leave. "Well, it's been nice meeting you, Mr. Stedman. I do hope you enjoy my pie." The polite words flowed effortlessly despite her embarrassment.

"We will—thanks again."

She nodded, turning away as the door closed. What a waste of time! Sitting still while Sadie curled her hair, fussing with her clothes, and all for nothing! She seethed all the way back to her house. Why had no one told her he was married? Sadie had known she was taking him the pie, and surely she knew he was married, since she was such good friends with Clay's aunt.

When she reached home, she left the buggy in her father's hands and went directly to the kitchen. Sadie had always been good to her, even if she did sometimes cross the line between employee and employer. Why would she let Mara make such a fool of herself?

"Sadie!" Mara called long before she reached the kitchen. The heat of emotion had brought the flush of perspiration to her skin, making her even more upset. She burst through the kitchen door where Sadie was preparing their dinner.

"What is it, Mara?" the woman asked with infuriating calm.

"What is it? I'll tell you what it is, Sadie Marshall! You let me go over there and make a complete ninny of myself— that's what! You knew I'd set my cap for Clay Stedman, and you made the pie. Don't tell me you didn't know!"

"Mara, I don't know what you're—"

"He's married and has a child to boot! Do you know how much time I wasted on my efforts today?" Mara paused to gather herself, realizing how unladylike she appeared. "Why didn't you tell me?" she demanded.

"Clay Stedman's not married, Mara. I don't know what you're talking about."

For the first time she wondered if she had it wrong. Maybe his wife was dead. "But the little girl—"

"Beth is his sister, Honey. Their folks passed on awhile back, and he's taking care of her."

Elation bubbled inside Mara, followed by the awkward feeling that she'd had a fit over nothing. She shrugged away the feeling. "She's his sister? He's not married? Are you sure?"

Sadie laughed. "Just as sure as shootin', Mara. Clay's come to take over the ranch now that his uncle's gone. He's not spoken for, and that's the truth of it."

Warmth flooded her limbs at her relief. She didn't know why she felt so drawn to the man—yes, she did. Who wouldn't be drawn to that tall, handsome, strong-looking man? He exuded confidence and power. She'd seen it in the way he handled the men around him at the dance. People were drawn to him, and he wasn't afraid to lead.

"I see that look in your eyes," Sadie said. "Don't you be out to hurt him now. He's a God-fearin' man with a good heart, and I don't want to see. . ."

Sadie continued, but Mara's attention turned to her first words. God-fearing men went to church. God-fearing men wanted a God-fearing woman. Her lips curled into a smile. Tomorrow was Sunday, and suddenly she had the worst hankering for the gospel message.

three

Mara suppressed a yawn. Why didn't they open a window in here? The heat held the air stagnant as the preacher droned on for what seemed like hours. She had arrived early, taking care to find an empty pew in case Clay wanted to sit with her. But old Mr. and Mrs. Furly took the seats to her left, and Sara McClain plopped down on her other side! Sara with a squirming two year old who had put her slobber-covered hands all over Mara's sleeve.

She straightened in the pew, trying to distance herself from the child. She didn't know why Sara had been so friendly lately. Indeed she had no reason to be, the way Mara had tried to come between her and Nathan when Sara had come to town. But who could have blamed Mara for the disappointment she'd felt upon losing her beau to a lowly mail-order bride?

The preacher was going on about a vine. Bittersweet was the name of it. Though Mara hadn't heard of it before, she could recognize from his description a vine she'd seen before. It was known for its beauty, with purple and white flowers and berries that turned bright red in late summer. The vine was beguiling but dangerous, the preacher said. Left unchecked it would take over a tree and strangle it.

When the preacher compared that attractive but deadly vine to sin in people's lives, Mara squirmed in her seat and distracted herself by toying with her parasol.

The preacher caught her attention when he asked them to rise for a word of prayer. *Finally!* Her back ached from the impossibly hard pew. Hadn't these people heard of upholstery?

She hoped to have an opportunity to speak with Clay afterward. He had come in with his sister and his aunt just before the service, leaving Mara with little choice but to wait.

17

"Amen."

The final word sent a shot of relief through her. Why in the world anyone would sit through this misery every week—

"Would you like to join us up at the spring for dinner, Mara?" Sara asked.

Mara looked at her and felt a momentary pang of envy at her petite beauty. "No, thank you. Maybe some other time." *Like when it snows in July.*

"Well, have a lovely afternoon." Sara turned and began gathering her belongings while Mara cast a quick glance around the back of the room. He was going to leave, and she was stuck between people who seemed in no hurry to leave!

She had turned toward the Furlys, hoping they would acquire a sense of urgency, when she heard his voice behind her. She froze. Had he come to talk to her? But, no, he was speaking with Sara. Mara opened her reticule and pretended to rifle through it while she listened.

"And we really need someone to cook for the hands and look after Beth for the two months she'll be gone," Clay was saying.

"Your aunt mentioned it a couple of weeks back," Sara said. "I'd be glad to pitch in, even keep Beth at our place while you're working, but I'm afraid I can't be away from our house right now. Hetty's back went out on her, and she needs constant care."

"I understand, Mrs. McClain. I'll keep that in mind, but I'm still hoping to find someone to stay with Beth at our place. Can you think of anyone else I might ask?"

Me, me! Mara's mind screamed.

"I can't think of anyone right off hand, but let me give it some thought."

Irritation flared like fireflies in her belly. Why didn't Sara recommend her? She was standing right next to her.

"So I'll see you in about an hour," Sara was saying. "Don't worry about bringing anything."

He was going with them to the spring! This was her chance to spend time with him. Ideas danced about in her head. She would do more than spend time with him today. She would convince him to give her the job. She could figure out how to care for a little girl—after all, she used to be one. And as for the cooking, well, she would simply get Sadie to do it.

Sara's family was leaving the pew, and Mara reached over to lay her hand on Sara. "I think I'll join your family at the spring, after all." She tried for a friendly smile.

Sara's eyes widened. "Why, that would be wonderful, Mara. You don't need to bring anything. I've cooked enough for an army."

Cooking—another chance to impress Clay. "Nonsense. I'll bring something—I insist."

She made her farewells and dashed back to her house.

"Sadie!" Mara called out as she hurried toward the kitchen. She hoped the cook would be in the middle of fixing lunch.

Mara flung open the kitchen door to find Sadie setting a pot of green beans on the stove.

"How was the service?"

"Long and boring. Sadie, I need a dish to take on a picnic." She browsed the array of foods being prepared and noted the sweet potatoes boiling on the stove top.

"You're going on a picnic?"

Mara ignored the skeptical tone. It was true she wasn't fond of the outdoors, what with the bugs and heat, but a woman had to make exceptions. She gestured to the potatoes. "Are those for your sweet potato casserole?"

"Well, yes, that's what—"

"Splendid! That would be just the thing." Everything Sadie made was wonderful, but that particular dish was a real treat. "When will it be ready?"

The taters will need to boil awhile yet, then I'll add in all the fixin's. I'd say forty-five minutes or so."

"Perfect." Mara turned to go.

"Why don't you come back in a bit, and you can help make them? I'll show you my secret ingredients." She winked.

"Oh, I haven't time. I need to change my gown."

She hastened from the kitchen and its heat before her hair wilted. Sadie wouldn't have time to fuss with it, and Mara knew she couldn't arrange it as Sadie did. She wondered what she should wear. Something stunning, yet not so hampering that she couldn't play with the children. Especially Beth. Why, by the time Clay tasted the casserole and saw how good she was with the girl, he'd be begging her to take the job. And if he didn't ask, she would simply offer.

Nearly an hour later Mara walked past the church and up the hill to the spring, her arms full. In one hand was the basket in which Sadie had placed the dish and, in the other, a dainty parasol. By the time she had climbed to the top of the hill, a fine sheen of perspiration filmed her skin. She stopped for a moment to rest. A part of her dreaded being in the company of Sara and Nathan McClain. It was awkward, what with their history, but Sara had been acting friendly lately, so she must not have hard feelings. Besides, it was Mara who had cause to be upset, the way Sara had come to town and snatched up the town's most eligible bachelor.

She picked up the basket and set off again, placing Sara firmly in the back of her mind. That was in the past, and today she needed to concentrate on impressing Clay. She wondered if he'd tasted the pie yet.

She heard the squeals of the children long before she cleared the cedars and saw the group. Clay and Nathan stood talking by the water while Sara and Beth set out the food on two quilts.

Mara neared the picnic area. "Yoo-hoo!" She waved as the friends turned to welcome her.

"I'm so glad you could come, Mara. It was nice having you in church this morning."

Mara retrieved the casserole from the basket and set it with the other food. A familiar-looking apple pie lay off to the side.

"You didn't have to bring anything," Sara said. "I declare, between you and Clay, we have enough food to last a week. He told me you made the pie. It looks scrumptious."

So it was her pie. Well, no matter. She settled on the blanket, holding her parasol carefully over her head. Clay and Nathan approached, and Mara realized her mistake. She shouldn't be sitting idle; she must show Clay what a hard worker she could be. She quickly turned and helped Sara set out the food.

Moments later they sat down to eat, and Mara nearly made another error when she lifted her fork before the prayer. Glancing around, she saw no one had noticed.

After the prayer the men ate the meal with relish while Sara cut up food for her little girl. She watched Beth gulp down her food and made a mental note to teach the child table manners.

"Oh, Mara, these sweet potatoes are delicious!" Sara said.

Mara felt a surge of satisfaction. "Thank you." She attempted a humble smile while the men seconded Sara's opinion.

Mara asked Clay about his hometown while everyone finished eating. He seemed more relaxed today than he had the evening before. Maybe he was succumbing to her charms.

Sara cut the pie, and Mara helped serve. She watched Clay take his first bite.

"Mmm, this is right tasty, Miss Lawton."

She felt a warm flush spread over her cheeks. "Thank you. It's my grandmother's recipe." Mara's grandmother, Sadie's grandmother—what difference did it make?

"I had no idea you were such an accomplished cook," Sara said. "What gives the pie that nice tangy flavor?"

Mara's fork paused on her plate. She took her time chewing the bite, stalling for an answer. Then she remembered seeing Sadie make the pie once. "I squeezed a bit of lemon juice over the pie before I laid the lattice crust."

Mara knew Sara was aware they had a cook. She wondered if Sara was suspicious. A glance at her face revealed nothing but friendliness.

When they finished eating, Mara helped Sara put away the leftovers while the men discussed roundups and birthing calves. Mara shuddered at the thought. When she'd finished her work, she was sorely tempted to stay and work her charms on Clay. But just then Beth announced she was going to look for tadpoles, and Mara stood. "I'll go with you." She tried for an eager tone.

Taking her parasol, Mara traipsed behind Beth along the bank of the water in silence. Beth removed her shoes and stockings. What did one talk about with a young girl?

"How old are you, Beth?"

"Almost nine."

"How do you like Cedar Springs?"

"There's one!" Beth waded into the shallow water, soaking her skirts up to her knees. She reached into the water with both hands, but the tadpole flitted away.

They moved on down the shore, making conversation as they went. The girl was rather sweet, even if she did behave in an unladylike manner. Mara could fix that in two months easily.

She kept Beth company while the girl frolicked in the water, keeping an eye on Clay as they rounded the spring to the other side. Between the food she had supposedly made and her efforts with the girl, Clay was sure to be impressed. Even though he sometimes seemed taken by her beauty, she sensed a certain aloofness in his manner. She wasn't sure why he was, but she hoped she could get beyond that cool façade.

By the time the two had made their way back to the group, Beth had taken Mara's hand, a sweet gesture that only helped Mara's cause.

Later, after lingering near Clay, Mara realized it hadn't occurred to him to offer her the job. No matter. She would simply volunteer to help as soon as she found the right time.

Her opportunity came moments later when Clay led his horse to the spring for a drink. She followed him, her face warming with the excitement of the challenge. From behind, his broad shoulders and narrow waist set her heart racing. When he turned, the sun silhouetted his profile, and his dark skin and hair reminded her of an Indian. She thrilled at the wild thought. Despite her mother's hatred of Indians, Mara had always found their wild, primitive ways fascinating.

Her parasol held high above her head, she waded through the tall grass toward him. Clay was everything a woman wanted in a man. Strong, handsome, confident. She would get this job and convince him she was the answer to his prayers, in every sense of the word.

four

Clay led Barnus to the water and turned to stroke his brown coat. He hadn't known when he had accepted Sara's invitation that Mara would be coming—he probably wouldn't be here if he had. She was comely—there was no doubt about that—but he couldn't let loose of the idea that she was just like Victoria. The way she used a parasol, the way she batted her long lashes—even the way she held her little finger out when she took a bite of bread.

That's why he was so surprised to see her take an interest in Beth. Pampered women like Victoria didn't cotton much to kids. They were only out for themselves. Why had it taken so long for him to see that?

"That's a fine-looking horse you have there."

He turned as Mara approached, her fancy dress caught up in one hand. "He gets me where I need to go."

"Your sister is a sweet little thing. I so enjoyed her company today."

He met her gaze, skepticism rising up in him. He was good at reading people—always had been. Either she was a good liar, or she meant what she'd said. "She's had a hard time of it, but she's coming around."

Out of the corner of his eye he watched her smooth out her gown. *Lands' sake! It must be hotter'n anything under all those layers. Maybe having all that skin exposed at the neckline made up for it.* Not that he'd noticed.

"I couldn't help but overhear when you were speaking with Sara earlier."

She paused as if waiting for him to nudge her on, but he remained silent. That was another little trait of Victoria's that had irritated him.

"It so happens I'm available for the next two months, and I'd be ever so happy to help out."

He looked at her then. Was she joshing? An overindulged lady like her looking out for a child? Cooking for fourteen men? Scrubbing the floor on her hands and knees? A picture formed in his head, and he tried to hold back the laughter that bubbled in his chest. It came out sounding like a snort, and he tried to keep the mirth from his lips.

Her perfect little mouth fell open, and she sucked in her breath. "You're laughing at me." Her back straightened, and her tiny chin tilted up.

He tried to collect himself. "I'm sorry. It's just—" Another picture flashed in his mind—of Mara trying to run wet clothes through a wringer and hold her parasol too. Laughter barreled through his chest and out his mouth. This time there was no stopping it.

"Well!"

"I'm sorry—I don't mean—" He couldn't seem to get a full sentence out around his laughter. He tried to imagine Victoria doing the day-to-day chores his aunt did. Why, he'd guess Mara didn't own one practical dress, much less—

"Would you like to explain what you find so funny?" Her voice quivered with anger. She turned to see if the others heard his laughter. She lowered her voice. "I was offering to help. How dare you mock me." Her eyes flashed with indignation, and her perfect lips had begun to form a not-so-attractive pout.

He sobered then. Regardless of his opinion of Mara he was not behaving as a Christian. He cleared his throat, letting his laughter die. "I'm sorry. You're right. But I don't think you know what you'd be getting into. You'd need to cook, not just for us, but for fourteen hands."

"I can cook just fine, Mr. Stedman. Why, you've tasted two samples of my culinary abilities already."

He had forgotten about that. The pie and sweet potato dish were pretty tasty. Still, there was the matter of caring for Beth and doing the house chores. He couldn't see it happening.

"Miss Lawton, come look!" Beth called from the side of the spring.

Clay watched Mara's face soften. "Just a minute—I'll be right there." She watched Beth play, the indignation falling from her face.

Clay wondered if he'd misjudged Mara after all. He was sure Victoria wouldn't have set foot in the kitchen, much less been able to turn out mouth-watering dishes. And she had never taken an interest in Beth or any other child. In fact, she'd often remarked about the inconvenience of having children underfoot.

And it wasn't as if anyone else was beating down his door. Maybe Mara's motives were pure. What did he really know about her, except that her family was rich? He felt a moment of guilt. Having money didn't make a person bad. Still, she couldn't be used to working.

Mara turned back to him, her eyes still sparkling with exasperation. "I'm not going to beg, Mr. Stedman. I'd thought to do you a favor, but—"

"I can't pay much." He named the amount he could afford, knowing such a paltry sum would seem like nothing to her.

She blinked. Whether surprised at the low wage or that he was actually considering her offer, he didn't know.

"I'm hardly doing this for the money."

"You'd have to fix breakfast for fourteen men and pack up a lunch for all of 'em too. They eat supper at the Coopers', but it'll still be a lot of hard work and long hours—"

"I'm perfectly capable."

Clay tried to look past her baby blue eyes and into her heart. Why was she doing this? Were her motives as pure as wanting to help out? Though she had used her wiles on him in their brief acquaintance, he didn't cling to the notion that she was serious. No, women like Mara liked to see how many men they could collect. It was not a good quality, but it didn't make her incompetent.

Mara arched her brow, her face bathed in amusement.

"All right," he said, resigned. He hoped he wasn't making a big mistake.

"You needn't seem so despondent," she said with a pout. "You'll see I'm remarkably resourceful." With that, she turned and paraded over to his sister.

He hoped she was right.

That evening, as Mara glanced through her latest issue of *Woman's Home Journal,* she wondered how she should handle her mother and father. Her mother wouldn't like the idea of Mara's hiring herself out, even for a couple of months. But if she could somehow convince her that she wanted to help out, perhaps her mother would go along with the idea.

One thing was sure. Letitia Lawton would never abide the idea of Clay as a suitor. Mara must approach the matter carefully. And once her mother was in her corner, her father would not be far behind.

A new gown from France arrived that afternoon, and Mara stood in the beautiful satin masterpiece, her mother fussing over the gathers and folds.

"Perfect! Oh, I knew this buttery yellow would look perfect on you!"

Mara agreed that the color brought out the gold highlights in her hair and complemented her skin tone beautifully.

"Perhaps we should host a party this summer and invite Doctor Hathaway. His heart would give way if he saw you in this." Her mother fluffed the hem.

"At his age his heart may give way anyhow," she mumbled.

"What, Dear?"

"Oh, Mother, don't you think the doctor is altogether too old for me?"

"Nonsense, my dear! Your father was no younger when we married. Really, Mara, you must give up this silly notion of love and romance. You must think about your station in life."

"I want both."

While her mother told of her own courtship and marriage, Mara allowed her mind to drift. She imagined being married to Clay. He would be owner of the Stedman spread one day and could certainly provide well for her. She shook her head. When did she begin thinking so seriously about the man? Why, she nearly had to beg him to let her work for him, much less get him to consider anything more serious.

But changing his mind would come easily once he was in her presence every day. What man would be able to resist a woman who cooked, cleaned, cared for his sister, and did it all while looking like a princess? She studied her image in the mirror. The man didn't stand a chance.

"Mother," she said when there was a break in conversation, "I've offered to help the Stedman family for a few weeks this summer while Martha Stedman travels out East."

"Help?" Letitia Lawton stood, her own blue eyes clouded in question. "Help how?"

Mara pretended nonchalance, smoothing the collar of the gown. "Oh, you know, keeping an eye on her niece, tidying up, cooking—"

"Why, Mara, you don't even know how to cook."

She turned to her mother then. "I thought perhaps I might ask Sadie to help a bit. Do you think it would be all right?"

"Taking over for Martha Stedman is going to be more work than you can imagine, Child! Why, your hands will get rough and callused, and you'll perspire all day long! What would ever drive you to—?" She stopped, her painted brows drawing together. "It's that nephew of hers, isn't it?"

"Of course not, Mother—"

"Now I know he's handsome, in a roguish, dark sort of way, but you mustn't be smitten by his looks. He's a simple rancher, not fit for—"

"I know—I know, Mother. That's not why I'm doing this—"

"Why, your poor aunt Millicent made the same mistake! Don't forget how she followed that cowboy all the way to North Dakota only to be burned alive in that shack of hers. Those savages!" Her mother pulled a handkerchief from a pocket and dabbed at the corner of her eyes. "Mark my words,

Daughter—if you let your heart rule your choices you'll live to regret it."

"I know, Mother. It's not Mr. Stedman I'm concerned with; it's his sister. She was at the spring yesterday, and I found her to be a delightful little girl. But she needs refinement. I want to take her under my wing."

"Well, there's no finer woman to teach her, my dear. But are you sure you want to put yourself out like this?"

"I want to do it. Can I ask Sadie to help me?"

Her mother puffed up the sleeves and adjusted the collar. "We'll have to pay her extra. Your father's been watching the funds very closely lately." Her brow wrinkled in thought.

"Father?" She'd never found him to be tight-fisted with their money. In fact, he was always willing to indulge his wife and daughter.

Her mother shrugged. "Perhaps there's a little financial glitch—I don't know—but you let me worry about your father. Go ahead and let Sadie know what you need from her."

Mara kissed her mother on the cheek. "Thank you, Mother."

By the time Mara went to bed, everything was all worked out, on her end at least. She knew her mother could handle her father. Sadie had agreed to make a huge breakfast in her own kitchen each morning, and Mara would deliver it to the Stedman ranch in the buggy. The noon meal Mara would handle herself. Apples, cheese—something simple the men could take with them. Then for dinner Sadie would come early, fix it, and be gone before Clay arrived. It was all settled. In less than a week the adventure would begin.

five

Mara sat down on the sofa, wiping her brow with her handkerchief. It was only nine o'clock in the morning, and it felt as if it were noon at least. She'd delivered the food Sadie had made—sausages, eggs, flapjacks, biscuits—but making the food had been the least of it! She was expected to serve the food, enduring the leers and comments of fourteen smelly cowboys. Then she had to pack lunches for them to eat on the range. She didn't take a bite herself until the men were gone, and by then she was too famished to care that it was cold.

And, for all her efforts, not one word of thanks.

When she and Beth finished eating, Mara took her first good look at the mess the men had made. Why, she had seen neater hog pens! Cold, congealed lumps of yellow egg littered the table, floor, and chair seats. Greasy fingerprints covered the long, sawbuck table, which was also dotted with sticky honey. And the napkins she had laid out so nicely sat in filthy wads wherever the men had dropped them.

In fact, she had been so busy serving that she'd scarcely said a word to Clay. When was she supposed to win him over if she had all this work to do?

She looked in dismay at the note in her hand. Mrs. Stedman had left her a list of chores she would need to do each week. The list went on and on! Mara didn't think she could get everything done in the two months she would be here, much less every week!

"Wanna play dolls, Miss Lawton?"

Mara smiled faintly. "I wish I could, Beth, but I have heaps of work to do." When she noticed the sad expression on the little girl's face, she added, "Perhaps you can be my helper. Would you like that?"

"I've already collected the eggs and fed the hogs. Can you teach me how to make bread?"

As soon as I learn how to myself. Mara gestured to the note. "Your aunt Martha says we need to—"

"You say that funny."

"It's not polite to interrupt, Beth. One should wait until—say what funny?"

"Aunt. You say it like 'Aaahnt.'"

"Yes, well, anyway, we mustn't interrupt. It isn't ladylike. Now we need to do the laundry straight away. Would you like to help with that?"

"I suppose."

She seemed less than enthusiastic. Mara couldn't blame her. She hadn't a clue where to begin. Oh, if only Sadie were here! Maybe Beth knew how. Still, she didn't want to admit her incompetence to the girl. What if she told Clay?

She would make it a game! Children liked games, didn't they? Surely Beth was no different.

Mara turned to Beth. "I'll tell you what. Why don't we see how much you know about chores? We'll make a game of it. You tell me what to do, and I'll do it. Kind of like Simon Says."

Beth smiled, clearly liking the idea. "All right. First, you heat some water on the stove."

Well, that was easy enough. Especially since the stove was already hot. They got a large pot and pumped water into it, setting it on the stove.

They gathered the soiled clothing; then Mara quizzed her pupil again.

"Next, we fill the tub with water," Beth said. She showed Mara where the tub was, and they took it outside and pumped it almost full of water. By the time that was done, the water had heated, and they dumped it into the tub.

"Next, we shave off some soap."

Mara retrieved the soap and knife from the kitchen and awkwardly cut chunks. Beth stirred the water with her hands until the soap dissolved, while Mara brought the laundry outside.

They continued along in the same manner. Mara scrubbed the clothing on the washboard while Beth ran clothes through the wringer and hung them on the line. By noon they were nearly finished, and the sun was beating down from high in the sky. Even in the shade the heat permeated Mara's gown, and she felt trickles of perspiration running down her neck and back.

Beth stood in the sun where the clothing line stretched across the yard.

"No wonder your skin is so dark," Mara said to her. "If you want fair skin like mine, you need to wear a bonnet."

Beth giggled. "Indian skin can't be light, Silly."

Indian skin? She stopped scrubbing and watched Beth clip a shirt onto the line. Of course! Why hadn't she seen it before? The dark skin, the black hair. It must've been Beth's curly hair that had fooled her. "You and Clay are Indian?"

"My ma was a full-blood Navajo." She tipped her chin proudly. "My pa was white like you."

Mara pictured Clay in her mind. His hair was black as soot, but it was clipped so short, and his eyes were not dark at all. She blinked at the wonder of it. Somehow that made him seem all the more attractive. Wild. Dangerous.

Her mother would be appalled.

She continued with the wash, lost in thoughts at her discovery. Her arms ached dreadfully. She pulled the last garment from the water, drooped it over the side of the tub and looked at her hands. They were wrinkled and red from the lye soap, and she wondered if they would ever look smooth and creamy again.

She barely had the energy to slice a chunk of cheese and some bread for a quick lunch. Beth, on the other hand, seemed full of energy. While the laundry dried on the line, they got out the butter churn, which Mara dropped on her toe. Pain shot up her leg, and it was all she could do not to howl in despair. She stifled a sob. She could do this, she told herself. She could.

They made butter, following Beth's instructions. Mara thought her little game was working beautifully until Beth looked at her halfway through the process.

"You don't know how to do any of this, do you?" The girl said it with such certainty that it caught Mara off-guard.

"Why, whatever do you mean?"

"The laundry, the butter—you've never done it before, have you?"

Mara cleared her throat and dropped the butter churn handle. She could either 'fess up and hope Beth didn't tell Clay or lie. She realized, too, that Beth could prove Mara was clueless by not giving her any instruction.

"All right—it's true." Mara gave her a wry grin. "I didn't think your brother would let me help if he knew the truth."

Beth stared at her for a moment. "It's all right. I won't tell."

Mara smiled warmly. "Really?"

"Really. And I can teach you how to do 'most any chore."

Mara stuck out her hand. "If you let me teach you how to be a lady."

A broad smile spread over Beth's face. "Deal!"

Mara breathed a sigh of relief. Hard as all this work was, everything was working out splendidly.

❧

This isn't working out at all. Clay had watched his hired hands get stirred up over Mara this morning. Not that he could blame them. She had been a sight to see, all gussied up and serving food that had melted in their mouths. Who'd have thought a woman who looked like that could whip up a breakfast of sausages and eggs with all the fixin's? A woman shouldn't be allowed to look that comely—that was all there was to it.

He had held his tongue as his men tried their best to win Mara's affections. It had put him in a foul mood all day. He didn't even want to think about why.

And if enduring breakfast wasn't enough, he had to listen to his men talk about Mara all day—until he finally told 'em to shut their traps. They had looked at him sideways, and

Clay knew he'd acted out of character. But at least they had changed the subject.

With the other cowboys having their supper at the Coopers' restaurant, he'd thought he was in for a peaceful night until he arrived home and found that Beth had invited Mara to stay for supper.

He watched her now from his seat as she put the food on the table. Her fancy dress looked a little worse for the wear, with dirt smudged here and there. As she spun away to fetch another platter, he noted her hair had come loose from its knot. It hung haphazardly down her back. Her shoulders seemed to have drooped a bit over the course of the day. And was that a limp she was sporting?

As she neared the table with a dish of green beans, he covertly studied her face. She looked different from this morning. Instead of her perfect hairdo, she now had little curly-cues framing her face. This morning's flawless skin was now flushed from the heat of hard work. But somehow she looked even better now.

She looked at him then, her hand pausing. Her lips parted, and her eyes seemed to ask a question. He was unused to this Mara. She seemed uncertain, vulnerable.

She blinked, setting down the dish. Her hand reached for her hair in a futile attempt to straighten it. "I must be a sight."

A sight for sore eyes. Clay scowled. Where had that thought come from? He tore his gaze from her, determined not to give her any ideas.

"What can you expect when you come to work all gussied up in a ball gown."

She stiffened, her lips tightening in a straight line. "I can work just fine regardless of what I'm wearing."

"It must be hot as blue blazes in that getup."

"As if it's any of your concern—"

"Your work is my concern—"

"What I wear isn't!"

"Fine, then—suit yourself."

"I will!"

Stubborn woman. If she wanted to fuss with a hot, heavy dress, who was he to care? Mara hurried back into the kitchen in a huff. Only then did Clay notice Beth watching from the doorway.

"You don't like her, do you?"

He sighed. The problem was, he was afraid he liked her too much.

"I think she's nice," Beth said.

Mara returned, setting down a platter of fried chicken, and sat in the chair opposite him. Clay avoided her gaze as Beth took his hand for prayer. Growling internally, he reached out to Mara's daintily extended one. Hers was warm and small, but firm as if she were still riled from their conversation.

"Go ahead, Beth."

Clay wasn't sure he'd be able to put two sensible words together. As Beth prayed, Clay determined to ignore the woman. If she was going to be around for two months, he'd have to keep to himself. He wasn't going to get all moony over another Victoria.

He ate the meal in silence, not even pausing to compliment Mara on the supper, which he had to admit tasted good. Instead, Beth ruled the conversation, eventually drawing Mara out.

"You really saw electricity?" Beth asked.

Mara finished chewing a bite of food. "Well, you can't see electricity, but I saw what electricity does. Just as you can't see the wind, but you can see it bending branches."

"Like God," Beth said. "You can't see Him, but you can see what He does."

"Uh, right. Father took us to New York when I was a little older than you to see the first neighborhood with electric lights."

"I don't understand how it works."

"It's very complicated but quite convenient. Electricity travels through a wire to your home and gives power to electric lights."

She proceeded to tell Beth the particulars of Ben Franklin's power station and direct current.

Clay was surprised at her knowledge of the subject. Not just her knowledge, but her ability to describe it in a way a child could understand. Victoria hadn't been able to tell East from West, much less describe something as complicated as electricity.

Moments later the subject had changed entirely.

"You're really part of the royal family?" Beth asked.

"Well, I'm a descendant of Queen Elizabeth, as is my mother." She flitted a glance at Clay. "I'm said to have inherited her intelligence." She smiled coyly.

"Do you have any jewels from the royal family?" Beth asked, wide-eyed.

"Beth, that's rude," Clay said.

"Mother does," Mara said, unable to resist answering the question. "She has an emerald necklace Queen Elizabeth wore in a portrait. I'll show it to you sometime."

"Is that how your family got to be"—she paused as if trying to remember the right words—"dirty rich?"

"Beth!" Clay threw his napkin on the table and scowled at his sister.

Mara tried to stifle a giggle.

Clay cringed, suddenly remembering where she'd heard the phrase.

"But, Clay," Beth said, "that's what you said to Aunt—"

"That'll be enough now!" he said.

"That's all right, Beth." She smiled at Clay. "The term is 'filthy rich,' though I'm not certain why anyone put those two words together."

Clay finished his meal in silence, sure that a flush had risen from the collar of his shirt.

❧

Mara got ready for bed that night at eight o'clock feeling more weary than she ever had before. How did all those rancher wives do it every day? She would find out soon, if this kept up. She was glad Sadie was doing all the cooking! Why, she had sat down only for meals today, without a moment of rest all day!

Tomorrow she would wear her lavender gown. The color made her skin look flawless, and the deep-cut neckline displayed one of her finest attributes, if she did say so herself. Dread curdled in her stomach at the thought of wearing all those heavy layers. She would perspire all day.

But no way was she going to change her manner of dress simply because Clay had told her to do so. What audacity! As if he had any say in the matter.

He had touched a nerve with his bossy attitude, but Mara admitted, if only to herself, this was one of his more appealing traits. He was a strong leader, a challenge. It both attracted and repelled her. That mix of emotions excited her. He was no boy like Daniel. He was all man.

She fell asleep with a smile on her face, right after her head hit her feather pillow.

six

Mara groaned as she got out of bed the next morning. Every muscle protested the movement. Her arms ached, and, oh, her back! She limped over to her armoire and opened the drawers, each muscle aching with the movement. It even hurt to breathe!

"Sadie—!"

She sat on the bed and waited for the woman to come and help her. How would she get through the day if every movement signaled pain?

"Sadie—!"

The door opened. "Mara, hush, Child! Your parents are still abed," Sadie said, closing the door behind her. "What's the matter?"

"My whole body feels as if it's been run over by a stage-coach—that's what's the matter!" She stifled a whimper.

"You need to get yourself moving. You'll feel lots better after you—"

"I can't move! It hurts too much." She put out her hands, still pink and now sporting a blister from sweeping the floors. "And look at my hands! They're ruined!"

"Now, Child, buck up." Sadie patted her shoulder. "Nothing good comes easy. You have a fine little girl waiting over there for you and a whole mess of fixin's cooking in the kitchen. "Here, I'll get your frock." She opened the armoire and reached in.

"But I can't even move!"

Sadie stopped and nodded her head, pursing her lips. "Well, I s'pose I was right then." She sighed. "I told Mrs. Stedman you wouldn't make it a week." She shut the cabinet and started to leave the room. "I guess Clay will just have to manage without—"

38

"You said what?"

"I told her you weren't capable of hard work like that. I don't know what Mr. Stedman was thinking, giving you the job—"

Mara stood, ignoring the ache in her limbs. "I can too do the work!"

Sadie turned in the doorway. "Well, then, Missy, you'd best get ready." She left then, shutting the door behind her.

✽

One week and three blisters later, Mara showed up at the Stedman house to find Beth sick in bed.

"She feels hot, and she's got a cough," Clay said before starting to eat the fried eggs with the rest of the men.

Mara hoped she wouldn't come down with it too. She checked on Beth while the others ate. She was sleeping, her body curled in a ball. The hair framing her face clung damply to her cheeks and forehead. She looked small and helpless. Mara had never nursed anyone, but her mother had always cared for Mara when she was sick, so she knew a little of what to do.

Poor child. She had no mother at all. Mara felt the girl's forehead, surprised that she didn't stir. Her skin burned against Mara's hand. A wet cloth would be just the thing.

After wetting a cloth, she sat on the side of the bed and dabbed the girl's face and neck. Beth stirred a little and opened her eyes. "I don't feel good."

Mara laid the cloth across her forehead. "I know, Darling. You just stay here and rest. I'll check on you often, all right?"

The girl nodded then closed her eyes and seemed to fall asleep.

It was a good thing Beth had helped her last week, or she wouldn't know how to do the chores. By the time she returned to the kitchen, the men had left for the day. She was clearing the table and had picked up the empty bacon platter when she remembered.

The hogs. Beth hadn't been able to feed them this morning. And she would need to collect the eggs. The weight of her tasks hit her heavily, and for a moment Mara imagined herself buried beneath the load of chores that awaited her. The dishes, the laundry, the mending, the cleaning. The work went on endlessly. Would there ever be a moment when she felt she was finished? As soon as she completed one task, another rose up in its place. How did these women bear it?

Filling the basin with water, she decided the dishes would have to wait until she'd collected the eggs and fed the hogs. She picked up the basket and set about gathering the eggs. Except for one hen that tried to hoard her eggs, the task went well. Feeling a tinge of accomplishment, Mara set the eggs on the table and went to check on Beth.

The cloth on her forehead felt hot, so Mara took it to the kitchen pump and doused it with cold water. Back in the room, she eased her weight on the bed and dabbed at Beth's flushed face. The child flinched at the cold cloth, stirred, and opened her eyes. Mara noted that a glaze of fever shone in her eyes.

Beth snuggled up to Mara, laying her head in her lap. Mara's heart caught at the innocence and vulnerability of the movement. She lifted her hand and began to stroke the child's hair away from her face. Then she laid the cloth over her forehead and cradled Beth in her lap.

Beth turned toward her, burying her face in Mara's gown. She mumbled something.

Mara struggled to hear. "What, Beth?"

The girl shifted, her body burrowing against Mara. "You smell just like Ma," she whispered then heaved a big sigh.

Mara's heart lurched then softened. She looked at the child's angelic face. Her tiny pug nose. Her long lashes, now sweeping the tops of her cheeks in sleep. Beth's breathing leveled out, and Mara knew she was once again asleep. For the first time in her life she had tender feelings for a child. For the first time she could imagine what it would feel like to have a child of her own. To be protective, to put that child ahead of her own desires.

For a long time she sat cradling Beth, enjoying the slight weight on her lap. Only when Beth shifted away in sleep and burrowed once again in her pillow did Mara stand. After rewetting the cloth, she turned her attention to her next chore.

The hogs. Ugh! She dreaded going out to feed those filthy beasts. She looked down at her shiny black shoes and sighed. They would be ruined. And she never should have worn her petticoats.

She had watched Beth feed them only once, and it looked simple enough. She filled the pail with the grain and carried it out to the pen. Most of the hogs lay fat and lazy in the slop, apparently not caring that breakfast had been delayed. But a few stood near the gate and seemed to be protesting the late arrival of breakfast.

Arriving at the fence she saw the pigs had nudged the trough into the center of the pen. So much for dumping it over the sides. Now she would have to walk through that muck.

Mara unlatched the gate and tried to force it open, pushing against one of the sows. "Move!" The hog snorted, its face covered with dry mud, but it remained rooted to the spot. No doubt held in place by the thick layer of muck.

She pushed against the gate, leaning into it with all her weight. "Move, you big, ugly beast!"

Several of the other hogs wandered over to the gate. "No, back! Shoo!" She leaned heavily into the gate, and this time Mudface budged a bit. Mara took advantage of the momentum, pushing with all her might.

There! She was through the gate, and she paused to catch her breath. Now if these other oafs would just move—"Get back! Shoo, shoo!" She made her way through the throng, trying to step only in the drier spots. Finally she reached the feeder and dumped the bucket of grain. The hogs gathered and began eating noisily, as if they were famished.

"Ugh! Filthy beasts." She tried not to breathe in the heavy odor.

She turned to walk away but was caught before she had taken two steps. She looked back and saw, to her horror, that one of the hogs was standing on her gown! She cried out with indignation and kicked at the hoof. The sow didn't move. "Move! Shoo, shoo!" She kicked again, loathe to touch the dirty beast.

The big pig wasn't budging. It was too busy stuffing its fat belly.

She gathered her skirt and pulled gently, hoping to ease it out. When that didn't work, she kicked at the hoof again. "Get—off—my—gown!"

She gave a final yank, leaning back for leverage. At the same time the sow decided to shift closer to the food.

With the weight suddenly gone from her skirt, Mara fell back into the muck. The mud splattered up, and she felt herself sinking into the wet, slimy earth.

"Aauughh!" she howled and then opened her eyes to survey the mess. Before she could take stock, she heard something.

Laughter.

She looked around the paddocks and barns. Her gaze slid by then came back to rest on the figure perched not fifteen feet away on the fence. Clay was clutching his stomach with uncontained mirth.

Anger boiled inside her. She struggled to stand up and realized her skirts had risen to her knees revealing her frilled bloomers beneath them. "Aauughh!" she howled again and flung the sodden skirts back down around her ankles before trying to stand again.

Clay continued to display unbridled mirth.

"Of all the"—her hand slipped in the mud—"nerve!" She turned over on her knees, knowing she would ruin her gown but not caring anymore. "Instead of standing there laughing like a"—she pushed to her feet, aware that her backside was sticking up in the air—"a complete nincompoop!"

"Hold on there, Fancy Pants, and I'll—"

She sucked in a breath of foul air. "Well!" She rose to her full height, albeit unsteadily. "You, Sir, are no gentleman! How dare you mention my—my—unmentionables!"

"No offense, Ma'am. I've never seen such fancy duds—"

"Will you stop speaking of them!"

He stepped near her and reached for her arm to steady her.

She swatted his hand away, her face flushing again at the mention of her undergarment. "And what were you doing spying on me?" She planted her muddy fists on her hips. "Your behavior has been most rude!"

"I was just—"

"And how dare you speak to me that way! A gentleman would have turned away—"

"I never said anything about being a—"

"A gentleman would certainly not have mentioned what he had seen."

His lips twitched, and she knew he was stifling another round of his insufferable laughter.

She whirled and started toward the house, her angry stride hampered by the mud that sucked at her feet.

"Now, Fancy Pants, I—"

"Ohh!" She turned and shot him a look, silencing him. Reaching the gate she finally broke free of the mud and welcomed the hard-packed ground. Her gait quickened, but her sodden skirts clung to her legs.

The last sound she heard before entering the house was the unrestrained laughter of Clay Stedman.

seven

Mara removed a chocolate from the box and popped it in her mouth, settling back onto her pillows. After the day she'd had, she deserved a treat. It had taken a long, warm bath to soothe away the trials and remove the layer of filth that clung to her skin. And candies from France were just the thing to take her mind off that impossible Clay Stedman.

What had ever made her think of him as a possible suitor? He was a brute! A cad! She pictured in her mind's eye the way she must have looked, sprawled in the mud, her skirts gathered around her knees, the bottoms of her bloomers exposed. Her face grew hot. Had she ever been so humiliated?

She recalled the way Clay had guffawed. The way he'd called her Fancy Pants. She clenched her teeth then roared with anger, throwing her pillow across the room. It hit the wall with a thud.

What an insufferable man! He had all the manners of one of those hogs she had been feeding.

So what if he did look like Adonis? So what if he did exude strength like no one she had met? He was unmannerly, frustrating, and entirely too stubborn. After she'd washed up as best she could, he had insisted on explaining his presence at the barn that morning. He'd followed her into the house and insisted he came back simply to make sure the hogs were fed.

So he did have an excuse for being present, but that certainly didn't negate the fact that he was unbearably rude. She'd nearly quit right there.

But then she heard Beth call feebly from the other room. When she checked on the girl, she found her still hot, her eyes shiny like glass. Mara remembered then how Beth had clung to her only an hour before and told her she smelled like her mother.

44

All fight went out of Mara. How could she leave now, when Beth needed her? Not just to nurse her back to health but to fill a void in her life. The child needed a mother, a woman to nurture her. Mara had never once considered herself the nurturing kind, but something in Beth drew her. Her innocent sweetness and vulnerability softened a place in her heart, and she knew she couldn't leave. At least, not until her aunt returned.

Mara placed another chocolate in her mouth and surveyed her hands. They were rough with calluses. She sighed. How careful she had been all these years to keep her hands smooth and supple, and they'd been ruined in the space of weeks.

She set the candy aside and walked over to her cheval glass. She turned her face this way and that, peering closely at her skin. Her gaze narrowed on a faint dot on her nose. She sucked in a breath. A freckle! Her eyes adjusted to the room's dimness, and she found another dot, then another. Three of them!

Dismay spread through her innermost being. Her flawless skin, ruined! Oh, why hadn't she been more careful to wear a hat?

"Mara—!" Her father called from somewhere downstairs, and she could hear anger steeped in the one word.

"Coming!" She stepped away from the mirror, admitting that at least her figure was still as perfect as ever.

She hastened from her room and down the stairs, anxious to see what had upset her father. She found him in his office. Her mother was sitting near him twisting her hands nervously in her lap.

Her father wasted no time. "Your mother informs me we have been paying Sadie to do your work over at the Stedman ranch. Is that so?"

Mara glanced at her mother. "Well, yes, Father, but only the—"

Clyde Lawton slammed his fist on the desk. "I cannot believe the two of you have conspired in this without my permission!"

"Darling, I—"

"That's enough, Letitia! I had thought to shelter the two of you from this, but it seems I was wrong in doing so. It's good you're both here, for I have something to tell you. I'll tell William when he returns."

Mara tried to read her father's gaze, to see past the anger. It was unlike him to interrupt his wife.

"Things are going to be different," her father continued. "There's been a–a change in our financial condition." His gaze fixed on the papers in front of him.

Mara exchanged a confused look with her mother.

"Some investments have fallen through—some rather large investments." Her father seemed to wither before her.

"What are you saying, Clyde?"

He sighed and tilted his chin upward. "We've lost money, Letitia—lots of money." His jaw twitched.

Her mother gave a brittle laugh. "Well, how much? It can't be that bad. Daddy's inheritance is still—"

"I've lost it! I've lost all of it! I'd thought to make a fortune, but instead I've lost one."

"You can't mean—it's gone? All of it?"

At her father's nod Mara sank into the chair behind her. What did it mean? They still had money. They owned the Carriage Works. They were the wealthiest family in the district.

"It would have been bad enough," Mr. Lawton continued, "if it had been only the nest egg from your father. But the business is not doing well either. With the crop failure last year we've lost a number of families. Business is down everywhere."

Mara cleared her throat. "What does this mean, Daddy?" Her heart sat in her chest like a brick.

Clyde Lawton looked at his daughter. "It means no more Sadie. It means no more dresses from France. No more fine furniture or frills or fancy chocolates."

Her father went on, but Mara stopped listening. No more dresses? No more Sadie?

"Really, Clyde. You can't be serious! We can't let Sadie go.

Why, how would we feed ourselves? You're just being dramatic. It can't be that bad."

Her father folded his hands on his desk. "I've given you the facts, Wife, and we will all have to adjust to them. As for the cooking, Letitia, you will have to learn how to do that yourself—"

"I can't—"

"You can, and you will! There is no choice. Sadie is not going to work for free, nor is anyone else."

Her mother stood and crossed to the desk. "How could you, Clyde? How could you lose all of Daddy's money?"

Her father's face turned red as he replied. Mara slipped from the room, suddenly feeling like an eavesdropper. Her parents' angry words followed her up the stairs.

Her mind felt frozen in some thick, slushy fog. Was it true? Had her father given them an accurate picture of their situation? Was their wealth truly gone?

She couldn't believe it—refused to believe it. How would they manage without Sadie? Surely Mara wouldn't be expected to cook!

A chilling thought spread through her. If Sadie was gone, who would cook for Clay and his men? She entered her room and sank onto her bed. Sadie would have to get another job, and even the salary Clay was paying wasn't close to what Sadie was earning now.

She glanced at the box of chocolates on her table, picking it up and tossing the last one in her mouth. Would there be no more chocolates? No more perfumes or trinkets? Panic settled over her, threatening to smother her. What would happen when her beautiful gowns grew old and tattered? What would she wear, if not gowns from France? Surely she wouldn't be expected to select from the homely calicoes at the mercantile! How could she face the people of Cedar Springs in such common clothing?

It would be humiliating beyond reason! Mara flung the empty candy box to the floor. The wrappers scattered across the carpet, and the box settled in a far corner. How many times had she left things lying on her floor only to find them put in their proper place the next day? With Sadie gone, she would have to pick up after herself at the very least.

Tears puddled in her eyes, and she gave them free rein to fall. She thought of all the times she had flaunted her wealth to the townspeople. She liked being the one who wore the prettiest gowns and being able to afford anything she wanted; she had grown accustomed to it!

Her thoughts returned to her job at the Stedman ranch. When would Sadie be leaving? Tomorrow was Sunday, and she would not be expected to work at the ranch. Maybe Sadie would stay on awhile, at least until Clay's aunt returned home. Otherwise she would be in trouble.

⸎

Mara watched as Sadie buckled her suitcase closed. She had stayed on through the week, but now she was leaving to live with her sister in Wichita. She had shown Mara how to bake a few things in the past week, but her thoughts were confused with all the information. How would she remember it all? And with Sadie gone how would she ever coax her hair into the intricate styles the woman had managed?

"It's not far, Child. Perhaps you can come visit me later this summer."

For the first time Mara considered that she was losing someone who had been around all her life. She had taken care of Mara, played with her as a child, given her advice. The fact that she had overstepped her boundaries many times now seemed inconsequential. "How will we manage without you?"

Sadie patted her shoulder. "You'll do just fine. Why, you've already learned how to do laundry, clean a house, and feed hogs! If I've learned anything about you, Child, it's that you can do whatever you set your mind to."

Mara sucked in a breath, her throat suddenly aching with a knot. Sadie reached out and embraced her, and Mara felt the tears she had held back sliding down her cheeks. Losing Sadie meant much more than she had imagined. She was losing more than her cook and caretaker, though that was bad enough in itself. She was losing a friend.

"Ready, Sadie?" her father called from the parlor.

"Coming." The woman stood back from Mara. "Good-bye, Mara. You keep up the good work at the Stedmans'. I have a feeling about you and Clay—"

Mara straightened her back and huffed. "I've changed my mind altogether about that man. He's insufferable, bossy, and stubborn."

Sadie laughed then winked. "Sounds like just the kinda' fellow you need." The woman picked up her cases and left the room, calling one last good-bye before she and Mara's father started the drive to Wichita.

After they left, Mara wiped her cheeks and checked the clock on the mantle. She'd better get going if she wanted to have breakfast ready on time.

"Will!" she called to her brother.

A moment later he stepped into the room. "Stop your bellowing, would you? I've rigged up the wagon like I said. It's waiting out front."

She rushed out the door and climbed into the buggy seat, snapping the reins. In her mind she rehearsed all Sadie had shown her. She would fix biscuits today with sausages and eggs. With Beth feeling better now, maybe the girl could lend a hand. She undoubtedly knew more about cooking than Mara did.

Her hands, clutching the reins, shook in anticipation. She had to pull off this meal. After all, Clay thought she had been cooking all along. And even if she wasn't interested in pursuing him anymore, she didn't want to earn his ire. She wanted to stay and care for Beth. The girl had won a spot in her heart.

When she arrived at the ranch, she was relieved to see that Clay was doing his morning chores. Beth had gathered the eggs and was feeding the hogs at the moment. How glad Mara had been to turn over that chore!

Checking to make sure the stove was good and hot, she set out the ingredients to make dough. After putting the sausages on to fry, she turned her attention to the biscuits. She poured flour, salt, and baking soda, hoping she'd guessed right at the amounts. Next she pumped water into a cup and poured it in slowly, stirring until it reached the proper consistency.

By the time she had cut the biscuits and placed them on the pan, she was feeling pretty good about herself. It was then that she smelled something burning. Oh! She turned and looked at the sausages. Without thinking she grabbed the handle.

"Ooww!" She dropped the pan, and the grease splattered. "Ohh!" She snatched up a fork and quickly turned the sausages.

Her heart sank when she saw the charred skin. Fiddlesticks! Well, she would just have to serve them burnt-side-down. Maybe no one would notice.

Turning back to the biscuits, she slid the pan into the oven, reminding herself she would need to turn them over halfway through. How long had Sadie said? Six or seven minutes? It was impossible to remember all the details the woman had given her. And it didn't help that the stove was notorious for cooking unevenly.

She set the table for fifteen and then retrieved the butter, jelly, salt, and pepper. What else? The drinks! With the milk set on the kitchen table, she began straining it the way Sadie had shown her. She had poured half the glasses when she remembered.

"The biscuits!"

She ran back to the oven and opened the door. "Oh, no!" She pulled the pan from the oven, this time careful to grab a towel first. Tears pooled in her eyes at the sight. There was no getting around the fact that they were burnt. She blinked back the tears. Where was Beth? She needed help! Clay would be in soon, and she still hadn't fried the eggs.

The screen door slapped shut behind her. "What's that smell?" Beth asked.

Mara turned to see the girl's wrinkled up nose. "Quick,

Beth—open the windows! And bring me the eggs!"

Mara scooped the sausages onto a platter, hoping they had cooked long enough. She grabbed an egg from the basket and tapped it on the side of the skillet, as she had seen Sadie do. The egg slid into the grease, popping and sizzling. She cracked open four more, enough to fill the skillet, then breathed a sigh.

"Uh-oh," Beth said over her shoulder. "The yolks broke."

Mara looked at the eggs, and sure enough, the orange yolks oozed into the white of the eggs, swirling until they set and began solidifying. Not the eggs too.

In the background she heard the men arriving in the next room. Chairs grated across the floor, and boisterous laughter floated into the kitchen.

As she scooped the last eggs from the skillet, she let herself feel proud that two or three of the eggs had remained intact. So what if some of them had broken open? They were still edible, after all. She straightened her back as she carried the platter to the table. Beth followed her with the sausages. She heard someone at the table mention the room's acrid odor as she returned to the kitchen for the biscuits.

଼

Clay attempted to slice through the sausage with his fork. The blackened skin was tough as leather. When he finally managed to slice off a bite, he speared it with his fork and brought it to his mouth. On its way his eyes caught sight of the pink insides. He held the piece away and saw that, indeed, the meat wasn't cooked through. He looked around the table; the other men were eyeing the food with disgust.

Well, he would have only biscuits and eggs. He reached for the biscuits and noticed that they, too, were burnt. He cast an annoyed glance toward the kitchen door. What in the world had happened to Mara's good cooking this morning?

He turned over a biscuit. Though the top was burnt, the bottom was just short of doughy. He bit into it anyway. His teeth connected with the stony exterior and stopped. Trying harder, he finally bit through the biscuit. By the time he had chewed and swallowed the piece, his jaw ached. He dropped the biscuit on his plate and started on his eggs.

Around the table he heard whispered grumbles.

"This ain't fit to et."

"These biscuits are hard as your head, Ike."

"I've seen finer slop in a hog's pen."

Clay clenched his jaw. Whatever had gone wrong in the kitchen this morning, he hoped it was fixed soon. His men worked hard and needed a good meal to start their day. They didn't like bad food. And neither did he. As he choked down the eggs, he decided he wouldn't confront Mara about one ruined meal. After all the fine meals she'd prepared, it was unfair to bellyache over one gone wrong.

❧

Clay took one look at the supper table and set his jaw. He'd never seen slices of bread that looked like that. They had holes the size of walnuts and a crust as thick and dark as his morning coffee. The greens looked like the muck floating on his pond. The only thing that looked decent was the pot of chili in the center of the table.

The house stunk of burnt crust and garlic. His stomach churned—whether from hunger or revulsion, he wasn't sure.

They took their places and joined hands.

"Your turn, Clay," Beth said.

Clay bowed his head. "Thank You, God, for this—food You've provided." His nostrils filled with the garlic-laced air. "We pray that You would bless it to the—nourishment of our bodies." *And help us not to expire from food poisoning.* "Amen."

They began the meal in silence. Clay bit into the bread, relieved that it was edible after he peeled away the crust. He couldn't bring himself to try the vegetable that was cooked beyond recognition.

He dished out a huge bowl of chili. Thank the good Lord for something decent to eat at the table. He was half starved.

Silence reigned. The kind that reeked of strained tension.

What was going on around here? Beth kept casting wary glances at him. Mara hadn't looked up yet, with her eyes trained on the food as if she ate alone.

He took a big spoonful of the soup and slipped it in his mouth. A few seconds later he spewed it out into the bowl. The sound seemed to echo through the house. He took a big gulp from his glass of tea, trying to wash away the biting taste. He may as well have bit into a garlic bulb.

Anger rose up inside him. One meal was one thing, but something was obviously going on here that he needed to know about. A man couldn't work all day on food like this. He was paying the woman, and he expected edible meals.

Clay tossed his napkin down, glaring at Mara, who still stared at her plate. "Beth, go to your room."

"But I—"

"Now." His tone left no room for argument.

The room was so silent that he heard each step she took on the stairs. When he heard her door click shut, he turned and looked at Mara.

eight

Mara had jumped when Clay spit the chili back into his bowl. Even then, though, she didn't look up. She knew he was angry and had sensed it even before the meal began. The silence only made things worse. Beth had helped with dinner, but she was only a child. Neither of them had ever fixed a meal on their own before this morning.

After they had surveyed the mess that made up dinner, Beth had clung to Mara.

"I don't care if you do cook bad, Miss Lawton. I don't want you to go."

Mara embraced her, patting her shoulder. "I'm not going anywhere, Honey. Maybe most of the dinner is ruined. But look—doesn't the chili look perfect?"

As Mara sat across from Clay now, she could feel the hostility aimed at her. So much for the chili. She gathered her composure as Beth left the room, taking steadying breaths but not daring to meet Clay's gaze.

"Suppose you tell me what's going on?"

Mara's gaze flitted by Clay's. The quick glance was enough to see that his handsome features were knotted in anger.

"What do you mean?" She tried for innocence and bit into the string beans. She made a valiant effort to keep the revulsion from her face. Land's sake! What had she done to these things?

"I can accept that a body might ruin one meal. But this is two meals in a row, and something tells me more is going on here than meets the eye!"

Mara let the silence hang. She moved the green beans around her plate. Her chair squeaked as she shifted her weight. What could she say? If only she could explain that she'd had a bad day. It would work, if she didn't know tomorrow would be the same. Try as she might—and she had tried very hard—she was no cook. She was going to have to tell him the truth.

She arched her back, squaring her shoulders, and met his gaze. "All right. I had some help with the cooking before. Today I didn't have any help, so things were a little off—"

"What kind of help?"

"There's no need to interrupt! No wonder Beth has atrocious manners—"

"Don't change the subject! Who's been helping you in the kitchen? I can't afford to pay anyone else."

"Who asked you to?" she said, her own anger seething beneath the surface. "Sadie was helping me, and my father paid her for it. Things would've been fine if we hadn't lost all our—" She stopped abruptly. The last thing she wanted was for the whole town to find out her family was no longer wealthy.

"Lost all your what?"

"None of your business!"

"It's my business when the meals around here taste like hog slop."

"Well—I never—!"

"I can tell you never—never baked a batch of biscuits, never fried a pan of eggs, never made a loaf of bread, and never made a pot of chili! What did you do, use every garlic bulb in the cellar?"

Fury and hurt welled up inside her in equal amounts. The two emotions teetered back and forth like two sides of a scale. She had worked so hard to learn everything. She had acquired calluses on her perfect hands and freckles on her flawless skin. She had even sliced her hand while cutting up those bulbs he had just mocked her about. That chili had taken her half the afternoon to make, and in one sentence he had taken all her hard work and thrown it in her face.

Her lips trembled. She tried to speak, but her emotions whirled in her head in a frenzy of war. In one motion she stood and spun away to the kitchen.

"I'm not finished yet!" Clay called from the table.

Mara let the door shut behind her and began pumping water into the basin. With the sound of the gushing water she didn't hear him approaching until he stood behind her.

"I can see where you'd need help, what with cooking for so many. Why didn't you tell me Sadie was giving you a hand?"

Her anger got the best of her. She turned to face him. The truth shot from her mouth with the force of bullets from a gun. "Sadie didn't help. She did it all. Every breakfast, every dinner, everything! She made the pie I brought you weeks ago and the sweet potato casserole I brought to the spring. I can't cook a lick, Clay Stedman—so there!"

❧

Clay watched Mara as she turned on him, wrath spilling from her eyes. Her face was flushed, her perfect mouth clamped tight—until she unleashed her anger. He blinked at the force of it. He heard all she said, confusion rising inside him.

Why would she have tried to pass Sadie's cooking off as her own? Even the pie she'd brought him wasn't her own. He frowned as she finished her tirade with crossed arms. Her chin tilted up, and fire shone from her eyes. The anger he had felt, the confusion her words had wrought, drained from him.

His gaze caressed her heated face. How could a woman look so beautiful with anger gushing from every pore? Her eyes were the clearest blue, like spring water flowing from the mountains. Her skin was creamy perfection, the heated flush giving her cheeks a rosy glow. His eyes fell on a faint smattering of freckles on her nose.

They gave her an air of vulnerability. She looked adorable, and despite all reasoning, he wanted to kiss her.

Her eyes met his, her expression softening as the gaze drew out. Probing. Questioning. Her lips parted then shut. They drew closer, and Clay wondered if he was leaning or if she was. He didn't care. All he cared about was the woman who was inches from him.

"Clay?" The door to the kitchen snapped open, and Clay jerked upright.

Beth stood at the threshold. "Can I finish eating now?" Her gaze darted questioningly between him and Mara.

Clay cleared his throat. "Yeah, yeah, go ahead."

She slipped from the room, and Clay cast a furtive glance in Mara's direction. He could feel the flush climbing from under his collar.

Mara sniffed, her chin hiking up, her posture drawing an impossibly straight line. She turned back to the basin and began washing a pan. "If you're going to eat, you'd best get to it. I'm not sticking around all night waiting on you."

Clay blinked. Was he, only moments before, about to kiss this woman? What in the world had he been thinking? She was the very kind of woman he had sworn to avoid. A wealthy, spoiled debutante. And now he could add lying to her list of faults. What had he been thinking? He gave a brittle laugh as he left the kitchen. That was the problem. He hadn't been thinking at all.

nine

What had she been thinking? Mara's hands, holding the reins, still shook. She was furious with him only moments before. How had one look changed her emotions so dramatically?

Her heart beat faster as she remembered the look in his eyes. He had been angry himself, and as Mara pumped water in the basin she was sure he was going to fire her. So, she'd reasoned, she may as well tell him the whole truth about Sadie. She had expected him to get even angrier at her deception. The last thing she'd expected was for his expression to soften. She had nearly drowned in the warm pool of his eyes.

He had been about to kiss her. And for the first time in her life Mara thought she might have allowed it. Many had tried, but she had always played coy and turned away. She had never wanted a man to kiss her—until now. She was sure he wouldn't have turned away if Beth hadn't entered the room.

How could she have wanted to kiss such an infuriating man? They had nothing in common. He worked a ranch; she enjoyed a life of luxury. He was religious; she wasn't. He was half-Indian; she was a descendant of royalty. He had no wealth; she had—

Well, she supposed they did have one thing in common. With their money gone, maybe they weren't so different after all. Still, her mother would have a fit if she knew Mara had almost kissed a half-Indian man. Why, if she married the man, her mother would have Indian grandbabies.

The thought caused a ripple of laughter to catch in her throat. Wouldn't her mother be fit to be tied?

The thought of marriage brought a jolt of reality. What was she thinking? As attractive as Clay might be, he was frustrating and stubborn. But, she had to admit, the man had integrity. She wondered if it had anything to do with his religion. Did his devotion to God cause him to be a man of his word, a man who treated his workers fairly, a man who commanded respect?

She remembered how unaffected he had been toward her from the beginning. Why, even her best charms and beauty hadn't worked on him.

At least she'd thought they hadn't worked. But, she reminded herself, hadn't the man almost kissed her? Perhaps he wasn't as unaffected as she had thought.

She felt a moment's satisfaction; then reason took hold. It didn't matter if he was attracted to her. She no longer wanted him, and she had a feeling he was already regretting the indiscretion in the kitchen. He had made it clear he thought her a spoiled child. And the way he continued to call her Fancy Pants rankled her.

She was glad tomorrow was Sunday, and she didn't have to work at the ranch. She could sleep late, laze around the house all day and, best of all, avoid seeing one Clay Stedman.

❧

The sound of a screeching voice woke Mara, and she rolled over in a haze of sleep, fighting the call of wakefulness.

"You owe me, Lawton!" The words slurred into her ears, and she unwillingly opened her eyes.

"I let you 'ave her—what'd I get in return?"

It was a woman's voice, Mara realized, and it was coming from outside. Curiosity got the best of her, and she slipped out of bed and peeked through her lacy curtains.

The plump woman staggered in front of the house. A bottle lay on its side at her feet.

"You don' wanna let me in—thas fine! Whas all the townspeople gonna think o' the way you cheated me?"

She bellowed the words so loudly that Mara was sure the whole town had already heard. What would such a woman want with her father? She was a worthless drunk. A movement to her right caught her eye, and she saw that the church crowd was letting out. The woman saw it too.

"See, now—'ere they come, Lawton. You don' pay up, an' I'm gonna tell 'em how you cheated me!" She gestured grandly and nearly stumbled backward.

Families were mounting their wagons, and several began walking home. They would all be passing by soon. They could probably hear the drunk even from where they were. Mara slipped on her robe and ran down the stairs. Where was her father? They had to get rid of this woman or be embarrassed in front of the whole town.

She ran toward her parents' room as the woman screeched outside. "They took my baby girl! And look 'ow they treat me! Won' even let me in—"

Mara raised her hand to knock as her father opened the door and rushed past her. "Daddy, what's—"

"Not now, Mara."

She followed her father all the way to the front door which he had left open in his haste.

"Hush, Edith!" her father hissed at the woman.

The crowd from church neared, and two women lingered in the street. Mara felt like sticking her tongue out at them. She could just imagine the gossip they would spread.

"They took her away and for what?" The woman lurched unsteadily on her feet, talking to the townspeople now and ignoring her father.

"I gave up my own seed and now look how poor they done left me."

"Hush, now, and I'll give—"

The woman spied Mara peeking from behind the door.

Mara froze under her icy blue gaze.

"Look! There she is! A real beauty I gave 'em and look 'ow they've treated me!"

Confusion warred in Mara's mind. What was the woman going on about? Why, to hear her talk, you would think she had given Mara to her parents.

The thought spun crazily in her head. She was half-aware of the townspeople driving by, hearing every word the woman said. They looked straight at Mara. She slammed the door shut.

It was the ravings of a drunkard. The woman was intoxicated; there was no doubt about that. But what if her words held the truth?

Don't be silly! she told herself. *My parents are Clyde and Letitia Lawson. I'm the descendant of Queen Elizabeth. Practically royalty. They didn't even know that woman.*

"Hush, Edith." Her father's words replayed in her mind like a buzzing fly.

Maybe she didn't know the woman, but her father clearly did.

In a cloud of confusion she walked up the stairs. It couldn't be true, could it? Her parents would have told her, wouldn't they, if they'd adopted her? She entered the room and walked slowly to the mirror. Scanning her face she looked for proof of her parentage and settled on her blue eyes. Dread snaked up her spine as she remembered the same blue of the woman's eyes.

Her breath caught. *No! It can't be!*

Snatches of memories clawed at her mind. The time she asked her father how she acquired her blue eyes when both her parents had brown. The time she asked about her birth, and her mother brushed aside her question. Little things that meant nothing to her at the time—but meant everything now.

She walked to the window. Her father had everything under control now. The crowd was dissipating. The woman staggered away, her hand clutching what appeared to be a wad of money.

He had paid her off then—paid her to leave them alone. But the damage had been done. She saw a little girl pointing at their house. People were staring, talking.

Mara didn't know which was worse. That she was likely the child of a drunk or that the whole town now knew.

The sting of it hit her hard, and her stomach clenched in knots. She blinked back tears. Everything had been taken from her. It was only a matter of time before people found out she had no wealth. And now her own parents had been taken from her.

She was a descendant not of royalty but of a pathetic drunk.

Sobs rose in her throat, but she stuffed them down. Everything she had ever believed herself to be was gone. Everything she had flaunted was false.

If she had untangled the woman's words, surely the church crowd had too. It would take no time at all for the gossip to spread through the town that Mara Lawton was the child of a destitute, delirious, drunken woman. Everyone would laugh. How would she face the town? She wished she could stay in her room forever. Who was Mara Lawton if not a wealthy descendant of royalty?

She peered in the mirror, wiping at the tear that had escaped. Even her beauty had been flawed by freckles and calluses. And with Sadie gone her hair would never look as it had before. Besides, other women were around who were nearly as pretty as she. Sara McClain, Cassy Cooper—she didn't have much on them.

And at least they were married! She was practically a spinster. True, she'd had proposals, but none she'd taken seriously. Now who would want her? Who would want a woman whose family was poor, whose mother was a drunk, and whose homemaking skills were virtually nonexistent?

No one, that's who. Even Doc Hathaway wouldn't want her now that her family had lost its wealth. She would become a spinster everyone whispered about behind her back. They would laugh about how boastful she used to be about her wealth, her ancestors, and her beauty. They would laugh about how poor and homely she looked in her homespun clothes.

How strange that the distant words of the preacher rose in her mind. *It is hard to believe how the beautiful bittersweet vine could be so dangerous. How could something so attractive cause so much damage?*

Mara wiped the words from her mind. She didn't want to think about the vine or how it sounded hauntingly like her. She didn't want to think about what she had done to others or how cruelly they would treat her once they knew her plight. But, for the first time in her life, Mara wondered if that wasn't exactly what she deserved.

ten

All day long Clay couldn't get Mara off his mind. He'd heard what that drunken woman had said after church. Anyone with sense could cipher her meaning. Was it just the mad rantings of a drunk, or was Mara her daughter? If it was true, he wondered if Mara had known or if it had come as a nasty surprise. Given what little he saw of her face in the doorway, he would guess it was a shock. Either way, the folks of Cedar Springs would no doubt have the juicy morsel spread far and wide within the week.

He clenched his jaw. It was a shame folks couldn't keep bad news to themselves. He had already heard tales of how Mr. Lawton had supposedly lost his fortune to some bad venture. He didn't know if it was true, but if it was, Mara had a slew of unpleasant facts to reckon with.

That had been one of the reasons he hadn't fired her for deceiving him. It seemed inconceivable that the highfalutin Mara Lawton might need the scant sum he paid her. But if the rumors were true—

He refused to dwell on gossip. Even if the rumors were untrue, it wasn't as if a line of women was waiting to take her place. And he needed someone to take care of Beth until his aunt returned. He wasn't sure how they were going to get decent food. Maybe Mara would get better with practice. He hoped sooner rather than later, or they'd all be wasted away by the time his aunt returned.

Beth was sitting beside him and paused between bites of bread to question him. "Clay, what was wrong with that woman?"

He took longer to chew his food. "You mean the one in front of the Lawtons' house?"

She nodded and took another bite.

He sighed. "She was drunk. People act funny when they've had too much corn whiskey."

"Like Lightfoot and Blackclaw?"

He thought of his mother's people, many of whom had turned to the white man's drink like a baby to milk. "That's right."

"Why was she talking 'bout Mara like that?"

"That's none of our concern, Beth."

"I know, but she acted like—"

"Mind your manners," he said more firmly than usual. She flinched, and he softened his voice. "Enough gossip'll be going around without us helping things along." And that was a fact. Between the rumors of lost wealth and this latest, the town would be making Mara pay for every boast she had ever made, every heart she had strung along.

Despite her uppity ways he felt sorry for her. She was about to get a strong dose of her own medicine, and it wasn't going to taste so sweet.

&

Mara woke with puffy eyes from yesterday's confrontation with her parents. She could hardly believe that everything the woman had implied was true. Snatches of the conversation came to mind.

"Edith used to be our maid. . . ."

". . .out of wedlock. . ."

". . .left on our doorstep. . ."

As if finding out about her parentage wasn't distressing enough, finding out that she was given away like cast-off clothing chipped away at her pride.

"How could you not tell me? How could you have lied to me all this time?"

"We did what we thought best. . . ."

"We love you as our own, Mara. . . ."

"You've always been my little princess. . . ."

Her father had said the last with tears in his eyes. Her mother had been distraught, nearly to the point of fainting, but

Mara couldn't find it in her to feel badly. They should have told her. They shouldn't have let her live a lie.

All the reassurances of their love did little to patch her wounded spirit. Her world was shaken—couldn't they see that? She felt as if her whole life had been a lie: the wealth, her royal heritage. Nothing she had believed about herself was true.

After slipping into a gown, Mara tried to arrange her hair. She knew better than to attempt to curl it, but perhaps it would look all right if she pulled the front up and secured it at the crown. She fumbled with the brush and clip. Her silky hair would simply not stay up. How had Sadie done it?

Frustration rose from deep within her, and she threw the clip across the room. Her hair hung straight down like curtains on each side of her face. She didn't even know how to braid it. Noting the rising sun just outside her window, she decided to leave her hair as it was. She had no one to impress this morning.

Still, her stomach clenched at the thought of seeing Clay again. Would it be awkward after the moment they had shared in the kitchen? Would he say anything about the drunken woman?

She fretted all the way to the ranch. Another breakfast to prepare. *Help me not to ruin it again.* The words popped into her head, and Mara wondered if they were in fact a prayer.

When she arrived, she began preparing flapjacks. She put water on to boil the eggs. Surely she could handle that. Maybe the men would be disgruntled with such a scant breakfast. She thought of the last fare. No, she was sure they would be relieved to have edible food—if she could make it edible.

She poured dabs of batter into the frying pan and watched them spread out into larger circles. So far everything was going well. Beth skimmed the milk and set the table while Mara kept watch over the flapjacks. She would not ruin them, she resolved, even if she had to stand there and watch them every moment.

She attempted to lift a corner of a flapjack to see if it had browned. She had to scrape against the bottom of the pan.

Oh, no, they are sticking!

She had lifted the corner enough to see that they were ready to be turned, but when she tried to pry them loose from the pan, they tore. She kept at it until all the pieces had been turned. But they were no longer circles, only torn shapes of various sizes.

"Beth!"

Moments later the girl approached.

"Why are they sticking to the pan?"

Beth looked into the black pan, now coated with a burnt layer. "Didn't you use any butter?"

"Butter?"

"It keeps them from sticking."

Relief seized her at the easy solution. Butter! She could handle that. "Bring it here, and will you put the eggs in the water too?" Mara scraped the remnants of flapjacks onto a scrap heap. She would start over and do it right this time.

Beth returned with the butter, and she coated the pan, letting it sizzle and pop before pouring in more batter. This time they turned easily.

A rush of accomplishment flooded her. She could cook. It was simply a matter of learning how. When she turned out the last flapjacks, the men began arriving. She looked at the stacks of golden cakes. They were perfect.

"Are you sure the eggs are done?" she asked Beth.

The girl shrugged.

Mara took one and peeled away the shell. She was determined to serve only good food today. She sliced through the egg white to see a beautifully set yolk. With a smile she carried the food to the table.

Later she realized she had been so busy that she had forgotten about her troubles.

⋙

That afternoon, as Clay was stringing barbed wire, his thoughts returned to Mara. He had wondered if she would sulk today, in light of what she may have learned about her parentage. But nothing in her demeanor gave that away. Clay had to admit, though, that he had been somewhat distracted as she served breakfast.

While his hired hands complained about having no meat for breakfast, Clay could only stare at Mara. Her hair hung in a straight, silky cascade to her waist. Gone were the curls and fripperies. No jeweled clips or spray of flowers. Just beautiful, golden hair.

It slipped forward over her shoulder as she was serving the meal, and he saw her tuck it behind her ear twice. The simplistic style gave her a look of vulnerability and youth. He hardly tasted the food, but it must have been all right.

Their eyes had met only once. She was across the table refilling Tucker's glass when her lashes raised, exposing her clear, blue eyes. He was taken away by her beauty. They looked at each other for a moment while Clay forgot about the others at the table. It was just the two of them.

When she overfilled Tucker's glass, her face bloomed in color as she dabbed at the spill on the table. She hadn't looked at him again.

⁂

Mara was feeling almost chipper after breakfast. Even the thought of having to do laundry hadn't put a damper on her mood. It wasn't until Beth asked an innocent question that the euphoria of success evaporated.

"Who was that lady at your house yesterday?" Beth continued wringing out the wet clothes.

Mara's hand stilled in the warm water. Should she tell Beth the truth? Brush over it with no detail? She recalled all the people who had stood near enough to hear the ranting woman. They knew the truth. It was only a matter of time before Beth heard the rumors. And she would rather the truth be passed about than the twisted versions some would think of.

"Well, I didn't know this until yesterday, mind you, but"— Mara paused to gather courage—"she's my mother."

"What?" Beth's brows drew together in confusion.

"You see, the woman—Edith—gave me to my parents, Mr. and Mrs. Lawton, just after I was born."

"She gave away her own baby?"

Tears threatened, but Mara gritted her teeth. She refused to shed another tear over this. "I'm afraid so."

"That's awful!"

Mara agreed with that. How could a woman carry a child for nine months and then give her away? She blinked back tears.

"I'm sorry," Beth said. "I shouldn't have said anything. Clay told me it was none of my concern."

So Clay had talked about it. He knew about it. She wondered if it had been pity she had seen in his eyes over breakfast. She would rather be laughed at than pitied. "It's all right. Everyone will find out anyway. Everyone will find out I have nothing." She scrubbed Clay's shirt.

"That's not true—"

"It is. You can't understand—you're only a little girl. I've lost my money, my heritage." She wrung out the shirt and tossed it in the basket at Beth's feet. "Even my looks are gone. Look at me! My hair is a stringy mess, my hands are red and callused, and I have freckles!"

"I think you're very pretty. And those things don't matter anyhow."

Mara gave a brittle laugh. What did a child know? She had no idea what it felt like to have lost everything, to be laughed at, and scorned by others. "You don't understand. I had enough money to buy anything I wanted; I had important ancestors—even a queen! What do I have now? Empty pockets and a drunk for a mother. Everyone is laughing at me now."

Beth wrung the shirt silently, and Mara thought she had finally made her point with the girl. But after hanging the shirt on the line, Beth returned to her side.

"Some people used to make fun of me because I'm Indian—especially when we lived in Texas. One time, Billy Joe and his friends threw tomatoes at me when I was walking to the mercantile. I cried all the way home."

"That's awful," Mara said, feeling a pang of sadness for the girl. What had Mara been thinking? People could be cruel, especially to different races. Her mind prickled with memories of the way she had treated some of the colored folk in town, ignoring them and snubbing them.

"When I came home, Ma saw how upset I was. Do you know what she used to say?"

"What?"

"She used to say, 'You're important and special. Why, you're the child of a King!' "

Mara frowned. Whatever was Beth talking about?

"You know—Jesus. I don't have to be white to be special. And you don't need money to be special. You're special because Jesus loves you."

Mara finished the wash in silence, and Beth seemed to sense her need for quiet. She wondered if it was true. Did Jesus love her just as she was? She didn't see how. She now had nothing to offer anyone, Jesus included.

eleven

Mara had never been to a barn raising. She stirred a pitcher of lemonade and looked around her at the swirl of activity. Men of all ages climbed on the skeletal frame like ants. Older men stood on the ground handing up tools to the others. She watched an adolescent boy shimmy up the boards as if it were nothing at all.

"Is the lemonade ready, Mara?" Sara asked from beside her.

"What? Oh, yes, here it is."

Sara filled cups while Mara set about squeezing more lemons. Her hand ached from the task, but it actually felt good to be doing something with the community. And the Farnsworths' were obviously thankful for the efforts of their neighbors.

Someone rang a bell, and moments later the men slid down from the frame and settled on picnic tables sprawled across the ground. The women served each man a plate heaping with fried chicken, mashed potatoes, and biscuits.

Mara paused after the last plate had been served, dabbing at the wetness on her forehead. She was thankful for her hat, which shaded her face, but the rest of her body sweltered under her skirts. She looked at the other women in their calicoes and envied their simplistic—and much cooler—dresses.

An awkward moment had passed when Mara first arrived. She was sure everyone else was staring at her. She even saw two young girls whispering and was certain they were talking about her. But, after that first moment, everyone returned to work as if she weren't there. She felt like the odd one out. All the other women had friends to chatter with, but Mara had no one except Beth. And she had gone off to play with her friends as soon as they arrived.

Mara felt shunned until Sara took her under her wing and showed her how to make lemonade. She even praised Mara's first attempt. Though how the woman could be so nice to her was beyond Mara. At one point she almost asked Sara how she could be so friendly after Mara had tried to ruin her new marriage. But Sara, seeming to sense where the conversation was leading, changed the subject.

Despite the envy Mara felt toward Sara, she had to admit the woman was virtuous. She wondered if it was because she went to church every Sunday like Clay.

"Come and sit, Mara!" Beth called from the table.

Mara noted that Clay and a group of young adults sat at the table finishing their meals. Happy at being included, Mara filled a plate and took a seat beside Beth. Daniel Parnell sat across from her with Lucy Derwin and Peg Hampton. Emily sat on the end of the bench as quiet as the town at dawn.

"What does your name mean, Clay?" Peg asked.

Beth whispered in Mara's ear. "Ma taught Clay about meanings of names."

"My whole name is Eyes like Clay," he said. "My ma said my eyes were muddy brown from the moment I was born."

"My full name is Margaret. What does it mean?" Peg asked from across the table.

"It means pearl," Clay said.

"My full name is Elizabeth, and it's Hebrew for Oath of God. Ma named me that because God always keeps His promises," Beth said.

"What about me?" Lucy asked.

"Hmm. I'm not sure about yours, Lucy—sorry."

"How about mine?" Daniel asked.

"I'll bet I know," one of the young men said. "Out of the lion's mouth."

Everyone laughed. Mara joined in, finally feeling part of the group.

"No, but it's a Hebrew name," Clay said. "It means judge or God the judge."

"How about me?" Emily asked quietly.

"Emily means beloved."

The girl blushed, and Barnaby asked Clay for the meaning of his name, but Clay didn't know.

Mara was keenly aware that she was the only one at the table who hadn't had her name deciphered. She took a sip of lemonade and wondered if she should ask. Maybe Mara meant "beautiful" or "noble." Surely her parents had picked a good name for her.

Gathering courage, she peeked around Beth to look at Clay. "What does mine mean, Clay?"

He paused, stopping his drink in midair between the table and his mouth. He opened his mouth and shut it again.

"Well, I—uh—"

Mara watched him expectantly as did the others.

He leaned toward her, ever so slightly.

"What? What does it mean?"

"It—uh"—he nearly whispered the words—"it means bitter."

Mara felt heat spread up her neck all the way to the tips of her ears.

"What?" Peg asked.

"It means bitter," Lucy said eagerly.

Mara heard the muffled giggles. She couldn't look at Clay or at anything else except the food on her plate.

She heard whispers mingling in with the giggles.

"It figures."

"Ain't that a hoot?"

"Serves her right."

Her stomach churned with humiliation. Why couldn't she have a nice name meaning like everyone else's? Why was everything in her life turning out wrong? She glanced around the table. She thought she was fitting in with these people and was finally being considered a friend.

She should have known better. They were laughing at her, as she had thought they would. They were glad she was no longer rich. They were glad she was born to a drunken wretch. They were glad her name was awful.

"Excuse me," she muttered, getting up on legs that felt weak. She hurried from the table.

"Miss Lawton," Beth called from the table.

But Mara didn't look back. She didn't have the nerve to look at the group that delighted in her humiliation.

ಜ

Clay had cringed when the group laughed at Mara. The fact that they were none too discreet about it angered him. He could have said he didn't know the meaning, but that wouldn't have been honest. Instead he had supplied all tne ammunition these people needed to give Mara a dose of her own medicine.

What was wrong with them? Hadn't they ever made a mistake? Weren't these the same folks he sat in church with every Sunday?

He slapped his hat on his head and stood with a scowl on his face that no one could miss. Without a word he left to find Mara.

"Clay," Beth called out, "can I—?"

"Let me handle it," he replied over his shoulder.

He walked around to the back of the house as Mara had done and stopped at the corner, but no one was there. Just a garden and a bunch of trees way out—

There—he spotted movement in the grove of trees. He set off toward the trees wondering what he would say to her. Well, first off, he would apologize for his part in it. His heart beat faster. He told himself it was because he dreaded the confrontation, but deep down he wondered if it was the compelling attraction he felt for Mara.

Entering the grove, he saw Mara sitting with her back against an oak. From the house she was out of view. She was leaning her head against the tree, with her eyes closed and her chest rising and falling quickly. The way she sat, hugging her waist with her arms and her golden hair cascading over her shoulders, Clay thought she looked like a little girl. His heart warmed.

He stopped, feeling as if he were intruding on her privacy.

When he cleared his throat, her head snapped around, and her eyes widened. He had expected tears but was relieved to see her face was dry. For a moment their gazes connected, and he saw sadness reflected in the depths of her blue eyes.

Then she turned. "Go away."

He shuffled his feet in the long grass. "I wanted to apologize."

"You've done it. Now go." Her words were lifeless.

He walked toward her and sank to the ground a safe distance away.

She looked to her other side as if she could pretend he wasn't there.

Clay plucked a dandelion and twirled it between his fingers. "I really am sorry." He shook his head. "I shouldn't have said anything."

She said nothing, just tilted her chin.

"I never thought they'd act that way," he said. "I've been scorned enough to know it doesn't feel good."

"That's different. You can't help being Indian. You didn't do anything to deserve anyone's contempt."

He frowned. "What do you mean?"

She looked at him then, and he saw the full anguish of her heart. "Don't you know I deserved it? I had it coming from every one of them."

"They still shouldn't—"

"I'm just like that vine the preacher spoke of—that bittersweet thing." She laughed grimly. "I was probably named for it. I've made a sport of strangling people and relationships. Take Peg. I stole Phillip Druery from her just for fun. He dropped her like a hot coal. And Emily. I used to tease her unmercifully about her appearance. I've been stringing Daniel along for two years, and I've snubbed Lucy more times than I can recall. Everyone hates me, and I don't blame them."

Clay grew still as Mara listed her transgressions. He wasn't shocked by her past behavior, but he was shocked by her brutal honesty. If she hadn't been before, she was aware now of the hurt she had caused. He tried to imagine Victoria broken the way Mara was and couldn't. Circumstances were prying away the hardened shell and exposing a surprisingly vulnerable woman.

Help me, God. Give me the words she needs to hear.

Neither talked for a few moments. Clay listened to the leaves rustling in the wind. He glanced at Mara. She picked at the frill on her sleeve.

Finally she spoke. "You probably know my family's money is gone. All of it."

He nodded.

"Did Beth tell you about my real mother?"

Beth had told him, but he had guessed it from the scene he witnessed in front of Mara's house. "Letitia Lawton is your real mother. She's the one who raised you."

She looked at him. "You know what I mean. I come from bad stock! My mother's a drunk, and there's no telling who my father is."

"None of that matters."

"That's all that matters!" Her brows formed an angry line.

"That stuff is all fluff and feathers. So you thought you had money and an impressive pedigree." He gestured toward the people who were helping raise the barn. "Are you any worse off than the rest of us?"

"Yes!"

"How so?"

She opened her mouth and shut it again. Her lips pressed together, and Clay noticed the flush climbing her cheeks. "At least you all can—can do something. I don't know how to do anything, I don't have any talents or abilities, and I can't cook a lick!"

Clay smothered a chuckle. "Those flapjacks and eggs were downright edible this morning."

"And I burnt the roast and ruined the bread for dinner!"

"They weren't that bad."

She rolled her eyes and huffed.

"Your worth isn't made up of what you do or what you have."

He saw the skepticism in her tilted head and pursed lips.

"What—you think it is?"

"Of course it is. Everyone knows the wealthy are treated differently and looked at with more respect."

"Maybe that's the way some people see it—"

"That's the way everyone sees it."

"And because you no longer have money or a fancy lineage, you think you have no worth?"

Her gaze fixed on her frilly sleeve. He could see he had made her think. Was that it? Was that the root of her sadness? The answer struck like a bolt from heaven. She considered herself worthless now. But didn't she know God looked at the heart and not at outward appearances? Didn't she know she was formed in God's image?

She didn't. How could she when she and her parents rarely graced the church with their presence?

"Do you believe in God?" He didn't know where the question came from.

Her head jerked around at the question. Her chin came up a notch. Ah, there was the Mara he had come to know.

"Of course I believe in God. I'm not a heathen."

"Then you believe God made you?"

Her eyes searched his as if wondering where he was going with these questions. "Yes, of course."

He paused a moment, seeing the deep sadness in her eyes. "How can you think you lack worth when the Creator of all things made you? Could anything our great God created be worthless?"

Her brows lowered, this time in thought.

"We're all made in His image. That's why we all have worth."

She blinked and studied her sleeve again as if lost in thought.

"All these people—" he gestured toward the men who were raising the barn and the women who were cleaning up after the meal—"do you think them—and me—worthless?"

She narrowed her eyes at him, clearly affronted. "How can you even ask that?"

Though she denied it with her words, Clay could see the realization on her face. She knew she had treated others as worthless because they had no wealth or position. And now they were her equal.

"I want to be alone now."

He stood, brushing the grass from his pants. "They'll come around in time, Mara, if you treat them with respect." He was silent a moment, letting his words sink in. "What you said about the bittersweet vine is true; I've seen it damage and kill trees. But it's not always that way. My mother used to plant it along our fences in Texas. It climbed up and covered them with leaves and flowers and those bright berries. In the fall she would cut the vines with their berries and fashion them into a wreath for the house. Even the bittersweet can be useful and serve a purpose." He stopped then, hoping he hadn't said too much.

As he walked away, he realized he had misjudged Mara. Perhaps she had been like Victoria, but her heart was changing before him. The vulnerable side of her drew him, but he knew he needed to be cautious. Despite her profession of belief in God, he was pretty certain the belief did not include a relationship with Christ. And until that happened, she was off-limits to him. He hoped his heart could remember that.

twelve

The next few weeks passed in a flurry of activity. With Beth's help most of Mara's meals were edible. She even turned out a tasty apple pie. Not as good as Sadie's, but she felt immense satisfaction over it regardless.

With Clay she found herself being rocked back and forth between frustration and admiration. One moment he was harassing her, and the next she would remember the gentle side he showed at the barn raising. She didn't know whether to hug him or slug him with a pot.

One night, after she had washed the dishes, she was walking through the kitchen door when Clay stepped through from the other side. The door nearly slammed into him.

"Whoa there, Fancy Pants! What's your hurry?"

"Stop calling me that!" she said, wishing the door had slammed into him.

"But it's fun."

"It's improper."

"Supper tasted good tonight."

She blinked at the change in topic then sniffed. So he had noticed her cooking had improved. "It was all right."

"I'm starting to miss that slimy green stuff. What was it—okra?"

She glared. "Green beans."

"And that freshly charcoaled taste on the dinner rolls—I'm starting to miss that too."

She huffed. "Keep it up, and that's exactly what you'll have tomorrow."

He laughed, but she sensed it was with her, not at her. As if he found her endearing. She noticed the way his eyes crinkled at the corners and the laugh lines around his mouth formed deep grooves when he smiled.

He stopped laughing, and Mara realized she was staring. She commanded herself to look away, but his eyes held her captive. It dawned on her then. He liked her. She could see it in his eyes. Sure, he was attracted to her looks. But it was more than that. He seemed to like her for who she was.

"I like your hair that way," he said softly.

Self-conscious, she drew her hand through the strands. She must look awful after sweltering in the kitchen all afternoon. But his eyes said differently. Her heart fluttered in her chest like a tiny bird's wings. Something stirred within her, something she had never felt before.

When he reached out and tucked her hair behind her ear, she felt the sensation down to her toes. He was going to kiss her, and every nerve in her body begged for it.

Please, please don't let Beth barge in this time. She stopped breathing, though her heart was booming like a drum. His gaze fell to her lips. She could almost feel the kiss already, the gentle feather-whisper of his lips on hers.

He blinked and straightened. Clearing his throat, he muttered something about a chore and disappeared out the door.

Disappointment spread through Mara like a disease. Oh, how she had wanted that kiss! She'd never wanted anything that badly, and the letdown was overwhelming. Why did he leave? She was so sure he was starting to care for her, but he'd turned away as if she meant nothing.

Suddenly, she remembered when other suitors had tried to kiss her. She remembered the times she turned away coyly, stringing them along like a marionette. Had Daniel felt this same keen disappointment when she turned away? Did he go home feeling rejected and miserable?

She saw clearly the way she had acted and hated it. Hated the way her eyes were open now to her behavior. It was a wonder anyone had wanted to kiss her at all.

But Clay had wanted to; she hadn't mistaken that. He changed his mind for some reason, but he'd wanted to kiss her all the same.

It would only be a few weeks before his aunt returned. The thought saddened her. She would miss seeing Clay every day, and she would miss Beth.

Mara sighed and began collecting dishes from the table. She would make the best of the time she had left here. Perhaps by the time his aunt returned, he would begin calling on her at her house.

ಜ

He couldn't continue seeing her like this. Clay ran a curry comb through his favorite mare's hair. Not that she needed it. But he'd had to get out of that house quick. If he'd watched her tuck that golden hair behind her ears one more time, he was going to grab her and kiss her. He nearly had tonight. Only one thought had kept him from it.

I need Your help, God. I know she's not one of Yours, but—

No. There were no "buts." She was off-limits to him. If only he could forget the vulnerable side he saw in her at the barn raising. If only he could think of her as he had when he first met her.

But he knew his first impressions were wrong. She may be like Victoria on the surface, but he could see a side of her now that Victoria didn't have. Mara had pluck. She was a persistent worker, and beneath that beautiful veneer lay a deeply vulnerable woman.

It was as if she knew all about her outward charms but knew nothing of her inward beauty. He wondered if any of her former beaus had ever seen past the beautiful façade. Had they glimpsed the inward beauty, or had they fallen for her based on her looks alone? He couldn't pass judgment on them. Hadn't he done the same with Victoria?

If he could make it through the next few weeks, he would be all right. Once he didn't have to see her every day, surely these feelings would go away. And maybe Mara would eventually become a believer. With all the changes in her lately, he wouldn't be surprised. *God, please use these circumstances to open her eyes to Your love. Help her to see herself as You see her, not as others see her.*

❧

"Fiddlesticks!" Mara said as the berry juice splattered onto her yellow gown. The stain seeped into the fabric, and Mara knew it would never come out. Why hadn't she put on an apron?

Beth grabbed a towel and dabbed at the spot.

"Another dress ruined." The week was not going well. Clay had been distant, not even baiting her as he usually did. She had cut her blue gown with the pinking shears, and it was beyond repair.

"By the time I finish my work here, I'll have nothing decent left to wear."

Beth gave up on the stain. "It won't come out."

"That's all right. I didn't think it would."

At some point she would have to go to the mercantile and select one of those frumpy-looking calicoes. To hear her father talking, though, they didn't even have money for that now.

"I don't know what I'll wear to the harvest social," she muttered to herself. She had worn all her nice dresses dozens of times, and besides they were too fancy for a harvest social. Her serviceable ones were the ones she had been working in, and most of them were stained or ruined.

"Why don't you make one?"

Mara laughed grimly. "I haven't the faintest notion how to make a dress."

"I do. I can help you."

Mara stopped stirring the preserves. "You can?"

"Sure. My ma taught me how."

Mara smiled her first real smile of the day. She could already do laundry, clean, and sometimes cook a half-decent meal. Now she would learn how to make her own gowns. And she had no doubt she could come up with prettier ones than the mercantile carried.

❧

Later that day, Sara McClain and Ingrid Manning stopped by, bringing a teacake with them. Mara served tea to the women while Beth went to play in the creek. Ingrid was far along in her pregnancy, and Mara could hardly help staring at the big round stomach protruding from the small woman. If she were ever that big with child, she would lock herself in her room for the duration!

An awkward silence filled the room after the cakes had been served. Why were they here? She hardly knew Ingrid, and Sara had no reason to be friendly with Mara. But, she admitted, that hadn't stopped her before.

Sara asked Ingrid about baby names, and Mara was grateful for the end to the uncomfortable silence.

"We're thinking Adam or perhaps Jonah. Which do you like, Mara?"

Mara was surprised Ingrid was even interested in her opinion. "Either one is very nice. What girl names have you selected?"

Ingrid laughed. "Cade is so certain it's a boy—he won't even talk about girl names."

"Isn't that just like a man? Nathan was so sure Caroline was a boy that he had me convinced too."

They went on to talk about the community and church, and before Mara knew it, they were asking her to come the following Sunday for Friend Day.

"Well, I—I don't know."

"Please? You can sit by me," Sara said.

"Or with me and Cade."

Mara remembered the last time she'd sat with Sara and her toddler and was glad for Ingrid's offer.

"We're having a picnic after church," Sara said.

Beth had been asking her to go as well. Maybe she could use a little help from above as she sorted out her problems.

"All right, I'll go," she found herself saying.

Ingrid and Sara smiled at one another. "Great. I'm so glad," Sara said.

After the women left, Mara and Beth weeded the garden. She didn't enjoy crawling through the dirt, but her dress was already ruined. What was a little dirt?

thirteen

Mara tried her best to pay attention to the minister, and she had to admit she did much better than last time. Of course, it helped that she wasn't sitting next to a rambunctious toddler. The message this morning was on Romans eight, verse twenty-eight: "And we know that all things work together for good to them that love God, to them who are the called according to his purpose."

Could that be true? Mara wondered. Could God use her family's financial predicament to bring something good into their lives? She thought of the story the minister had shared of Joseph and how God had used his brothers' evil deed and made it good. *Can You do that in my life, God?*

Almost before she knew it, they were standing for the final prayer. Some of the women had brought their food with them, but since Mara lived in town, she ran home to get the chicken and sweet potato pie she'd made. She hoped they tasted all right. They looked normal enough, though the chicken appeared a little soggy.

When she returned to the church grounds, she placed her food on the table. Two other platters of fried chicken already sat on the table. They looked crisp and perfect. So much for her chicken.

She turned from the table and had a moment of indecision. Whom would she sit with? She scanned the grassy hillside for a familiar face. She found Beth, but the girl was with her friends and Mara could hardly fit in there. She saw Sara, Nathan, and their little girl under a big oak. She stopped. She couldn't sit with them; it would be too awkward.

Ingrid! She was sitting all alone in a prime spot under a leafy elm. No sooner had she started walking toward her than she saw

Cade crouch down beside her and plant a kiss on her cheek.

She would rather eat alone than interrupt two lovebirds. Mara picked a spot a distance away and spread out her quilt. A line had formed at the food table, but she was in no hurry to eat.

Feeling terribly alone on the expansive blanket, she began wishing she hadn't come. She didn't have a friend in the whole town, unless she counted Sara and Ingrid. And she hardly knew them.

It hadn't bothered her before, because she rarely went to community events without her parents. When a party or a quilting bee was held, she wasn't invited, but she hadn't minded. She had considered the townspeople beneath her.

She gazed around at the groups of people clustered here and there on the hillside. They were laughing and talking and having a fine time. *Oh, why did I come to this silly picnic anyway?*

"Hey, there, Fancy Pants—is there room for me?"

Mara was torn between frustration at his greeting and relief at his appearance.

"Suit yourself."

He stood beside the quilt. The musky, soapy smell that was all his drifted her way. Her mouth went dry.

"Good to have you in service today," he said.

"I've been before, you know."

"No need to get your bloomers in a knot. I know you—"

"Will you please refrain from mentioning my"—she lowered her voice to a hiss—"my undergarments!"

He laughed and offered to get her a drink.

Mara watched him stroll away. He had the build of someone who worked with his hands all day. Broad shouldered, narrow waisted. She wondered why some other woman hadn't snapped him up.

After Clay returned with glasses of tea, they chatted about Beth and the ranch. When the food line grew shorter, Mara and Clay approached the table. She felt safe in his presence. Though she knew no one would harm her physically, she felt she could handle any social rebuffs as long as Clay was at her side.

Mara wondered what everyone was thinking of her and Clay being together. She had attended many functions with any number of beaus, so she decided they probably thought nothing of it.

Clay moved aside to let her in front. Most of the dishes were nearly empty, so she took a small sample from each dish, taking care to save room for her fried chicken. She saw to her dismay that the other two platters of chicken were empty.

"What did you bring?" Clay asked her.

She pointed to the greasy chicken and took a piece for herself. At least most people didn't know she'd made it.

She saw Clay take two pieces for his heaping plate. They each took a slice of her sweet potato pie, and Mara consoled herself that at least the pie had turned out.

As she and Clay ate, they talked about his aunt and parents, who had died of cholera. He told her about his mother's people, the Navajos. His father was a missionary when he met and fell in love with his mother. Clay made Mara laugh with stories of practical jokes he and his ranch hands played on one another.

As they talked, Mara discreetly watched Clay. When others walked by their spot, they stopped to say hello to him. He was obviously well-liked and respected already. She wondered if the people knew he was half-Indian. Now that she knew, it seemed obvious. His thick, black hair, though short, was as dark as the Indian daguerreotypes she'd seen. His skin was dark, but no more so than some others who worked outdoors. His eyes were the biggest foil, their grayish hues—

Mara realized suddenly that Clay had stopped talking and was watching her stare at him. By his look she could tell her admiration had been apparent. She was sure the flush of pink was blooming in her cheeks even now. Did he know how her feelings toward him had grown? It was no longer the crush she'd had at the beginning, before she knew him. Now he had taken root in the deepest places of her heart. She remembered the compassion he showed her at the barn raising. He spoke then as if he truly thought she was special—as if, even without her money and royal heritage, she was still valuable.

Clay cleared his throat and looked away.

Mara felt bereft all of a sudden. As if a cold wind had blown through their grove. She knew he must care for her a little at least. Why else had he almost kissed her twice?

Almost. Why had he turned away each time? He'd wanted to kiss her; she saw it in his eyes. If she could answer that question, she would be well on her way to having what she was starting to want above all else—Clay Stedman.

❧

The next day she and Beth made a trip to the mercantile to purchase fabric and notions for the dress they would be making. She was in fine spirits as she thought of having a new gown and hoped that, with Beth's help, she could fashion a beautiful one.

With her own money tucked in her reticule she opened the door. The bells on the door jingled in welcome, and Mrs. Parnell came out of the back room.

"Miss Lawton." She nodded her head in greeting. "What can I help you with today?"

She wore that cautious look people had been giving her for weeks. As if they expected her to bite them. Mara wondered again if she had been so mean that people had steered clear of her.

"I'd like to look at the fabrics, please."

Surprise lit the woman's eyes. "Why, of course. We have a new catalogue in, too, if you'd care to look at it."

"No, thank you—I'll be making a gown myself." The thought gave her a hint of pride.

"Well, the material is back in the corner." She pointed the way. "You let me know if you need help."

"Can I look at the candy?" Beth asked, holding up the two pennies Clay had given her.

"Yes, go on." Mara walked around the corner to the little nook where the fabrics were shelved.

She shook her head. How many varieties of calico could there be? She sorted through the stacks in hopes of finding something elegant and special. Some of the fabrics she recognized as belonging to various women of the town. She could picture them in their shirtwaists as she sorted through the bolts.

The bell on the door jingled as customers entered. Mara scarcely noticed as she discovered a lovely pale blue organdy. She held it next to her skin, admiring the way it enhanced her coloring. And with her blue eyes, it would— She stopped mid-thought when she heard her name.

"Peg said Clay Stedman sat with her at the church picnic," Mara heard one woman saying from the other side of the corner.

"Honestly!" another woman said. "Men are so blind."

"Not so. If they were blind, they wouldn't be enamored with her."

Both women laughed, and a heavy weight settled in Mara's stomach. Her skin prickled with heat.

"Well," one of them said, "you know he can't be after her money."

"Is it true then?"

"William Lawton told Peg, and she told me. Supposedly their father lost it in some investments." Her voice lowered to a whisper. "But some people think he gambled it away."

Mara's blood boiled at the outright lie. Her father had never gambled.

"How will Mara ever do without her fancy dresses and hats?"

"At least we won't have to hear her boasting about her ties to Queen Elizabeth. You did hear about the drunk who claimed to be Mara's mother, didn't you?"

"I heard. And I think it's highly amusing. Serves her right for being so persnickety."

Dismay and humiliation filled Mara. Is this what everyone was thinking of her? She wanted to melt right through the floorboards.

"Hello, Mrs. Parnell—I'd like five pounds of flour, please," the voice said.

"Surely, Miss Guilding."

Mara turned and saw, to her dismay, that the two women had approached the counter. If they turned, they would see her, and she desperately wanted to leave unseen! It was humiliating enough to hear the things they said, but for them to know she heard—

Footsteps approached, and she held her breath. *Please, God.*

"Are you ready, Miss Lawton?" Beth rounded the corner, and at the same time the two women at the counter turned.

Time froze, as did the expressions on their faces. Mara looked away. Her face heated, and she wanted nothing more than to disappear.

"Time to go, Beth."

"But you haven't—"

"Come along." She dropped the bolt of fabric, took hold of Beth's arm, and steered her out of the store. She could feel the women's gazes boring into her back. Worse yet, she could hear their laughter echoing the bell's tinkling as they exited the store.

fourteen

Mara fussed and fretted the next day. Hearing the gossip at the mercantile had been beyond humiliating, and she couldn't help but wonder if everyone in town was glad her life was falling apart.

After eating her mother's food on Sunday, she was eager to get back to the Stedman ranch the next day where she could at least produce edible food. Not delicious—it would probably never be that—but she could now make a palatable meal.

Tension had grown between her and Clay, making every encounter something she both dreaded and anticipated. She'd never meant to fall in love with a rancher, but she knew it was happening. How else could she explain the way her heart fluttered each time he walked through the door and the way her gaze wanted to caress the planes of his face?

She was no innocent when it came to dealing with men. She could read the longing in Clay's eyes. What she didn't know was what held him back. In the past she would have used her feminine wiles to coax him, but now it seemed dishonest and false. But without her former artifice she was lost. What did other women do to draw the men they loved? What tools could they use if not the batting of eyelashes and the flip of a fan?

After supper that night Clay went out to check on an injured horse. Beth, who had come a long way in acquiring manners, excused herself and went off to play with her doll.

Mara dried her hands on a towel and slipped out the door. When she rounded the house, she saw that Clay had rigged her carriage. Even though she had learned how to do it, she appreciated his thoughtfulness. Suddenly she realized she'd never thanked him for the kind deed.

Dusk had descended, and she knew she should be on her way. But when she saw the open barn door, she felt almost as if someone had lassoed her and was pulling her toward it.

Her heart hammered at the mere thought of him. Her nerves tingled with anticipation. She disliked the uneasy feeling in the pit of her stomach. She had never been nervous around other men and wished she had the composure she used to have. Only weeks ago she would have known what to say and do. Why, when it mattered so much, had conversation become so difficult? And how could she feel love for a man who frustrated her so?

She entered the barn and saw Clay kneeling at the front of a chestnut horse. The dressing lay in coils in front of the horse's hoof. He had lit a lantern for extra light and hung it on a peg. The yellow glow illumined his face, casting shadows in the hollows of his cheeks.

She watched him for a moment. He murmured softly to the beast. Her heart ached with want. What if he never loved her as she did him? How would she bear it? She remembered how she was before her family had lost so much. She was callous; she knew that now. But it was so much easier then. It hurt to be real. It hurt to be vulnerable. It hurt to risk loving someone.

Just then, as if sensing a presence, he looked up and saw her in the doorway. Their gazes caught and mingled in a dance of passion.

Without breaking his gaze he stood slowly.

She couldn't remember why she had come. Whatever it was no longer seemed important.

The horse whinnied, breaking the silence, and Clay turned toward him, stroking his shiny coat with a strong, deft hand.

"What's his name?" Mara asked.

Clay ran a hand through his hair. "Dancer."

"Will he be all right?"

"Should be fine in a couple days." His voice sounded raspy, and she wondered if his mouth was as dry as hers. "It was good to see you in church yesterday." He knelt down again and began applying a salve.

"I enjoyed the picnic especially."

His jaw clenched, and the shadows shifted on his cheek. "How'd you like the sermon?"

Back to that. She sighed. "I didn't understand parts of it."

He looked at her then. "What parts?"

She walked toward him. "He said everything ends up being good for God's children, or some such comment. I saw what he meant in the story of Joseph, but I don't see how God could bring good out of my family's situation."

"Your loss of wealth?"

She made circles in the dirt floor with the toe of her boot. "It's not just that. Mother's bitter and resents the cleaning and cooking she has to do now. She's hardly speaking to Father, and the strain is palpable."

"And you don't see how God could turn that around?"

She examined his eyes, their gray depths flickering in the lantern light. "No."

He rewrapped the horse's wound. Silence permeated the building. Wasn't he going to tell her she was wrong? Wasn't he supposed to tell her how God could change their circumstances as He had Joseph's?

Clay patted the horse's leg and stood. His eyes shone with something she couldn't pinpoint. "May I pray for you?"

She blinked. "Now?"

He nodded once, his gaze boring into hers.

"In a barn?"

He chuckled, his rich laughter teasing a smile out of her.

"What?"

He reached out and clasped her hand, drawing her to his side. "God is everywhere, not just in church."

"I know that but—" She had never prayed with anyone before. She'd heard Sadie praying aloud before, but Mara couldn't say she herself had ever uttered a real prayer.

He pulled her to a bundle of hay, and they sat side by side. He bowed his head, and she followed.

"Father, I pray that You'd be with Mara's family. Things don't look good to them now, as things must not have looked good to Joseph when his brothers sold him into slavery. I know Your Word says 'all things work together for good' to those who love You and are called according to Your purpose. It's hard to see through these confusing days what You might be planning for Mara's future. Please open her eyes to the good work You're about to do in her life. It's in Christ's name we pray, amen."

Did he expect her to pray too? She peeked and saw his head raised, his lips curved in a gentle smile.

"Amen," she said.

He squeezed her hand then let go.

She stood, and he did too. "You'd best get going."

She nodded, feeling as though her head were spinning in a frenzy. The words he'd prayed touched her heart, her soul. Could God really do as Clay had asked? She fervently hoped so.

He walked her out to the buggy and helped her into the seat.

"See you tomorrow," Clay said.

"Good night."

Mara was halfway home before she realized she hadn't thanked him for hitching up her buggy.

❧

Clay watched Mara disappear down the long drive. He took a deep, shaky breath. Mercy, what that woman did to him, to his heart. She was changing before his eyes, whether she realized it or not.

He thought of the Mara he had seen at the barn social. It seemed so long ago. Her façade covered a very vulnerable woman; he knew that now. And the shell was peeling away. Maybe Mara couldn't see the work God was doing in her, but he could. How else could He change Mara but to strip her of all the crutches she had depended upon? How else would she know she was valuable, not because of what she had and to whom she was born, but because Jesus died for her?

He shoved his hands in his pockets. But until she recognized and accepted what Jesus had done for her, she was beyond his reach. He thought of how she looked moments ago, the glow of the lantern flickering over her face. He smiled when he remembered her shock at his offer to pray in a barn. For all her fickle, feisty ways he knew his heart was on a downward slide to a valley that wasn't his for the taking.

❧

The next day Mara and Beth made a second trip to the mercantile for the dress material and notions. This one was uneventful, much to Mara's relief. Once they were back at the house, Beth showed her how to measure herself and make a pattern for the gown. Even with her other work, by late afternoon they had the pieces cut out and ready to baste together.

Supper was a silent affair. Clay didn't seem inclined to make conversation; indeed he didn't even make eye contact. So Mara coached Beth on the rudiments of table manners, quizzing her about the flatware settings as they went.

Beth took a spoonful of soup and brought it to her lips. "Like this?" She sipped the soup.

"Sip from the side of the spoon—like so." Mara demonstrated, and Beth followed. "Very good! I'll have you ready for any dining event before long. You could have tea with the queen and impress her with your manners."

"You'll have to teach me how to curtsy first," Beth said, giggling. "Can we go to the creek tomorrow, Miss Lawton?"

Mara smiled. "How did we get from curtsies to creeks?"

Beth shrugged. "I don't know."

"How far away is it?"

"About a mile, I think," she said.

"More like four or five, Beth," Clay said. "You'll need to ride."

"Can we?" Beth asked.

"Well, I don't know. I've never saddled a horse before," Mara admitted.

"Clay can show you how, can't you, Clay?"

"Well, I suppose I can. . . ."

"I'd like to learn how," Mara said. "Then I can ride anytime I need to."

"Let's wait until tomorrow, though. I need to fix up Dancer's leg tonight."

"Aww," Beth complained.

"Tomorrow's soon enough," Mara said. "If we can do it in the morning, we'll still be able to go to the creek tomorrow."

"Yippee!" Beth exclaimed.

They continued through the meal, though Clay remained silent. Mara realized she hadn't ruined any of the food tonight. A flush of accomplishment rose inside her. Maybe she wasn't ready for the county fair contests, but she could at least serve an edible meal now. On the other hand, her mother's meals were taking weight off William and her father.

Beth excused herself and took her plate to the kitchen.

Clay rose quickly, as if afraid of being alone with her. " 'Night, Mara," he said as he stepped through the door.

"Wait." Mara's thoughts froze. She didn't know what she wanted to say, but she wanted this wall of silence to come down. She wanted him to look at her as he had the other night. Aware that the moment was stretching awkwardly, she asked, "How's Dancer's leg?"

"He's on the mend. Going to check him now."

The urge to go with him was strong. She was about to suggest it when he pulled the door closed. "Good night."

The door clicked into place.

fifteen

The next morning Mara served breakfast without much trouble. The hired hands even complimented her on the biscuits and gravy. She knew they weren't as good as Sadie's, but the men were starting to appreciate food that was at least edible. She also noticed they didn't ogle her anymore. Perhaps they had decided they preferred a more domestic woman. But she had seen Clay shoot darts with his eyes at Tanner and B.J. whenever they made insolent remarks. Her heart told her it was because he was jealous, but surely he knew she was interested in him alone.

Beth was disappointed when Clay didn't have time to show Mara how to saddle a horse. They wouldn't be going to the creek today, but he promised he would take time after supper to show her how.

Mara wondered if he was stalling. Lately he had avoided her and even looking at her. She searched for reasons why. Was he repelled by her lack of womanly skills? Maybe he was only attracted to her beauty. Maybe he was put off because she came from bad stock. But hadn't he said at the barn raising that she had worth because God had made her and cared enough to die for her?

Maybe he plain didn't like her. The thought made her stomach clench painfully. She hadn't been very likable when he first met her. But she'd changed some, hadn't she?

Oh, this changing business was painful! At times she wished she could go back to being sure of herself, to not caring what others thought of her. But it was too late now. Her eyes had been opened, and there was no going back.

Later that day Mara tried on the gown they had basted, and she was pleased it fit. It looked plain, devoid of adornments, but she would add those later. The beautiful blue fabric was almost as nice as the fabric in the dresses she used to order from France.

By the time she slipped out of the gown, she needed to start supper. Mara anticipated the time she would spend with Clay tonight. If Beth stayed behind, they would be alone in the barn. Would he kiss her then? She thought she would faint from disappointment if he didn't. She had turned away many other men. She'd never wanted their kisses, and they had been eager to give them. And now that she'd finally found someone she cared for enough to kiss, he didn't want to!

When they gathered around the table and joined hands for prayer, Mara could feel her palm growing damp. His hand felt so big and strong that it nearly swallowed her own.

Clay was quiet throughout supper, and Mara wondered if he would find an excuse not to teach her how to saddle a horse. When Beth finally asked about it, he did exactly that.

"I'm not sure about tonight," he said. "By the time Mara finishes up in here, it's dusk. I can't let her ride home in the dark."

Mara's heart sank, not only because she'd looked forward to it all day, but because he apparently didn't want to spend time with her.

"I know!" Beth said. "I'll clean up in here while you help her."

"Well, uh, I don't know—"

"That's a splendid idea, Beth," Mara said. "Then we'll surely be able to ride to the creek tomorrow."

Beth clapped her hands in excitement. She ate the few bites left on her plate hurriedly and excused herself. Mara had never seen her so eager to clear the table. She took Clay's plate before he'd eaten his last bite.

Mara stood with her plate and glass, but Beth hastened in from the kitchen just then and snatched them from her. "I'll take those!"

Mara looked at Clay who eyed her warily. "All right, all right." He stood up and led the way to the barn.

She followed him, admiring the strong line of his shoulders, the narrowing of his waist, the long legs that covered the ground in big strides. She doubled her pace to keep up with his.

In the barn he lit a lantern for extra light and walked over to check on Dancer. Mara stood by the stall as he rewrapped the leg and then patted the horse on the neck.

"Which horses should we take tomorrow?" she asked.

He looked around the building, and his gaze fixed on a brown horse. "This is Ellie," he said, walking over to the horse. "She's gentle enough. We'll saddle her up, and you can ride her tomorrow." He opened the stall door and led her out. "Elizabeth rides Poncho, over there." He pointed to a spotted horse a few stalls down.

"First thing you need to do is put on a halter." He took one from a peg in the tack room and demonstrated. "Then you have to tether her to a rail." He tied a quick knot. "Next you'll need to groom her." He brushed the horse with the curry comb. "If any dirt or burrs are under the saddle and girth, she'll get sores."

Mara watched him carefully so she could do it on her own tomorrow.

After he groomed Ellie, he draped a blanket over the horse's back and smoothed it flat. "It's also important not to have any wrinkles or buckling so the horse doesn't get any sores." Next he retrieved a saddle from the tack room.

It was a standard saddle, but she assumed he would know she didn't ride astride. "Clay, I need a sidesaddle."

His brows pulled low over his eyes. "I don't have one."

She sighed. "Are you sure?" She'd seen the tack room before, and it was packed with all kinds of horse gear.

"This is a working farm, not an equestrian school."

Frustration welled up. She didn't feel it was proper for a woman to ride like a man. "But I've never ridden astride."

He heaved the saddle onto Ellie's back. "Well, you're gonna learn, I guess." His words were flavored with irritation.

She clenched her teeth. "I'll bring one from home then."

He turned and shot her a look. "That's fine and dandy, but I don't have a sidesaddle here for you to practice on."

Beth had her heart set on going to the creek tomorrow. If she brought her saddle then, Clay probably wouldn't have time to teach her until after supper. "Fine," she said coolly. "I'll ride astride."

She watched his jaw clench as he turned away. She didn't know why he had to be so snappy with her. Through the remainder of the lesson his instructions were short and abrupt. Her frustration with him mounted. How could a man she loved irritate her so much? He acted as if he'd rather be dragged by a bull than spend a moment alone with her.

When he finished tightening the saddle straps, he slipped his fingers between the girth and the horse. "You should just be able to fit three fingers in here. If you can't, it's too tight." He adjusted the saddle to check for positioning then began taking it off.

Mara was surprised at how many steps one had to take simply to saddle a horse. She wasn't sure she could remember it all. She watched Clay carefully undo his work. When he removed the saddle and started back to the tack room with it, Mara was caught off guard. Wasn't he going to let her try it by herself?

"Wait," she said.

He turned, his face lined with reluctance.

"Aren't you going to let me do it next? While you watch?"

"Can't you remember everything?"

Her chin came up a notch. "There's a lot more to it than I thought."

He mumbled but brought the saddle back and laid it by her feet. Without a word he took off the halter and blanket and shoved them into her hands.

The horse had already been groomed, so she skipped that step. She glanced at Clay and then dropped the blanket on the saddle and stepped to the front of the horse to put on the halter. When she was finished, she looked at her work with pride. She'd done it right. Next she placed the blanket over the horse's back, remembering to smooth out any wrinkles.

She turned to pick up the saddle. Ughh! She lifted it, straightening her back, and wondered how she could hoist it up onto the horse's back. She stood a moment, the weight of the saddle pulling on her arms.

"Well, are you just gonna stand there growing roots or—"

"It's heavy!" She took a deep breath and heaved the saddle on the horse, arching it through the air until it fell on Ellie's back. The horse staggered under the sudden weight. *Sorry, Girl.*

"Be careful!"

"I'm trying." She glared over her shoulder. The man had no patience.

She maneuvered the saddle into place, relieved to have landed it there at all. Then she noticed the blanket was rumpled under the saddle from its awkward placing.

"You need to smooth out those—"

"I know!" She lifted the saddle and fixed the blanket and then noticed the saddle was out of place. Her arms, weak from the lifting, couldn't seem to pick up the saddle again. She grunted with the effort, knowing she couldn't slide it or she would muss up the blanket again. She stopped, breathing heavily, her head falling forward as she caught her breath.

"Here, let me—"

"Just let me rest a minute, and I'll—"

He stepped close behind her, reaching around her shoulders. "You're stubborn as a mule," he said as he lifted the saddle easily and set it in place.

Exasperated at his remark, she spun around to let him know. Her mouth opened, but the words wouldn't come.

He was right behind her, his face a breath away from hers. She watched his expression change from anger, to surprise, then to something much warmer. She wondered if her expression underwent the same alterations. Shadows danced across his face as he clenched his jaw.

The anger drained from her. She'd hardly had time to catch her breath, but her lungs seemed unable to take in air. She could almost hear her heartbeat in the sudden stillness, and she smelled the soap Clay had cleaned up with before supper and his own musky scent.

His hands still rested on the saddle behind her. It was almost an embrace. If he would only slip his hands down to her shoulders. She longed for it. Her gaze caressed every line of his face, and she forgot how frustrated he sometimes made her. She remembered how gentle he was at the barn raising and how encouraging he was at the picnic. She remembered how protective he was with Beth and, yes, even her, when dealing with his ranch hands.

She saw the longing in his eyes, but something held him back. She saw his defenses go back up a moment before he turned away.

Keen disappointment filled her. Why? Why wouldn't he kiss her? Why did he back away from each encounter? "Why?" She didn't realize she'd spoken the word until he looked back at her.

ða

He weighed her question and his answer. Mercy, how he'd wanted to kiss her. Her eyes had begged for it, and it had taken every bit of resolve to turn away. But nothing had changed. She was still as lost as she'd been last week. *Help me, Lord. I can't tell her the truth.* "You'd best finish up here if you're going to leave while there's any daylight left."

"I'm not leaving until you answer."

"It's nothing. Now you'd better—"

"Something is making you turn away from me."

He counted the planks in the ceiling. She couldn't make him answer, no matter how stubborn she was about it.

"Don't you find me—comely?" Her head lowered as if afraid to meet his gaze.

His stomach tightened at the vulnerability he'd seen in her eyes. Two months ago she wouldn't have asked such a question. Now she was questioning everything, even her beauty. He longed to put her fears to rest—to quench the self-doubt that stirred in her heart. "Of course I do." She still refused to meet his gaze. "It's just—"

"I'm finished!" Beth scurried through the door and stopped, eyeing the two of them with curiosity. "Can you do it now, Miss Lawton?"

"I—" Mara's voice was rough, and she cleared her throat.

"She can do it," Clay said. "I'll hitch up your buggy." As he turned, he heard her retort.

"Don't bother." Her voice was laced with irritation.

Stubborn woman. He would do it anyway, whether she liked it or not.

sixteen

Two days later, just as she finished with the breakfast dishes, Sara came by on her way to Ingrid's house.

"Cade sent for me a bit ago," she said from her wagon seat, her words rushed. "Ingrid's time has come. Cade says she's afraid. Would you pray for her?"

Sara was asking her to pray? "Why, yes, I'll, uh—sure I will."

"Thanks!" Sara snapped the reins, setting the horses in motion. "I'll let you know when the little one arrives!" she called as she sped away.

"May I pray with you, Miss Lawton?"

She'd forgotten Beth was at her side. "Certainly."

They sat on the porch steps, and Beth took her hand. They bowed their heads, and Mara waited for Beth to pray. Silence spread awkwardly around them, and Mara realized Beth was waiting for her to pray. She cleared her throat.

"Uh, God? Ingrid's time has come, and well, I guess You know that already. She's afraid, so please calm her down and—and help everything to go all right." Her mind blanked, so she ended the prayer. "Amen."

Mara peeked at Beth, but the girl's eyes were still closed, and she began praying.

"Jesus, please keep Mrs. Manning and her baby safe. Help her know You're with her all the time and not to be afraid. Help Mr. Manning not to faint the way Clay did when I was born—"

Mara stifled a giggle that rose in her throat.

"And help Doc Hathaway do everything right. Amen."

Mara squeezed her hand, and they looked at one another.

"Did Clay really swoon when you were born?"

"Uh-huh." Beth giggled. "Ma said he walked in when he

wasn't s'posed to and keeled over."

"My! I hope Mr. Manning doesn't do that."

"He's a grown-up. He knows he's not allowed in the room."

"Well, that's true enough." Mara stood and stretched. "Well, we've got a heap of work waiting, so we'd better start."

The day dragged on. Would they ever hear how the birthing went? She wondered if it would be a boy the way Cade thought. What would it feel like to share such an experience with the one you loved? She couldn't imagine anything more special than having a baby that was a blend of you and the one you loved. She wondered what a baby of hers and Clay's would look like. Would he have dark hair and skin like his pa? Would he have Mara's blue eyes?

She shook her head. She shouldn't even be thinking like this. The man wouldn't even kiss her, much less—

She heard a wagon approaching and looked up from the garden where she was pulling weeds. Dropping the straggly plant in her hand, she walked to the front of the house.

It was Sara. Mara could see even from where she stood that Sara's eyes were puffy and bloodshot.

Dread ripped through Mara. "What—what is it?"

Sara pulled the reins as the horses drew to a halt. "It's Ingrid." Tears swelled in her eyes and tumbled down her pale face. "She—she's gone." Sara covered her face with her hands, her body quaking with sobs.

"What do you mean?" She couldn't mean Ingrid had—

"After she had—the baby—she just kept—bleeding." The words were choked out between sobs. "We did everything we could, but she just kept—"

Her words stopped as realization sank into Mara's heart. "The baby?"

Sara wiped her face. "The baby's fine. It's a sweet little boy." Her lips turned up in a wobbly smile. "Ingrid got to hold him, before she—" Sara looked at her. "She knew. She knew she was dying. And she had such peace." More tears spilled down her cheeks. "She kept saying to Cade, 'You have to let me go.

Jesus is calling me home.' " Sobs wracked her body again.

Mara reached up and took Sara's hand. "Do you want to come inside?"

Sara squeezed her hand. "Thanks, but I need to get home to Caroline."

"I'm so sorry, Sara. I know you were close." Mara felt her own eyes stinging with tears. "Ingrid was a special woman."

Sara nodded. "Pray for Cade. He's beside himself."

"I will."

Numbly Mara watched Sara ride away. She had hardly known Ingrid, but the woman had reached out to her, knowing the terrible things Mara had done. Ingrid was a godly woman. She didn't deserve to die so young. And what about this baby that would grow up without a mother? *Why, God? Didn't we ask You to keep her safe? Why didn't You answer?* A lump lodged in Mara's throat. How could Ingrid have such peace about dying? Why wasn't she angry at being cheated out of life? That's the way Mara would feel.

She looked up at the sky as if she might find God there. *If You're there, God, and if You care at all, please help Cade. He's going to need it.*

❧

The weather was exactly as it should be for a funeral. Gray overcast skies looked ominously dark beyond the bright fall foliage. The wind whipped angrily at the leafy branches and swept across the deadened grass, tugging at skirts.

Mara looked at the mourners gathered around the hollow spot in the ground that would soon house Ingrid's body. *It isn't fair. What did Ingrid ever do wrong? She was a sweet, unassuming woman who cared for others. If anyone deserves to be lowered into that pit—*she stopped the scary thought. If the thought of her body rotting in the ground didn't terrify her, the thought of what lay beyond the grave did. The words Ingrid had spoken on her deathbed played over and over in her mind. *"You have to let me go. Jesus is calling me home."* Mara knew she wouldn't have been at peace if she had been dying. She would have been terrified.

Pastor Hill stepped forward, a somber expression on his weathered face. "Today we gather to mourn the loss of a dear friend, wife, and mother. Yet, in our faith, we also celebrate her home going."

Folks around her nodded their heads in agreement. How could they be so secure, so sure there was a heaven? So sure they were going there when they died?

The words of the minister faded to a distant hum as Mara's gaze settled on Ingrid's husband. Cade stood beside his brother on the gently sloping hillside, a tiny bundle cradled in his arms. She could hear the baby's fussing over the rustling of the leaves. Wind whipped Cade's hair in front of his face, but he did nothing about it. Sara, at his side, whispered something and held out her hands, but Cade shook his head.

The minister was talking about heaven now and reading from the Scriptures. "But as it is written, 'Eye hath not seen, nor ear heard, neither have entered into the heart of man, the things which God hath prepared for them that love him.' " He looked up at the people gathered. "Ingrid Manning loved the Lord—you know that. And God has already prepared a place for her, for all of His children. A place that is beyond our imaginings."

He looked at Cade. "I know we have questions in our hearts. Why did our Father call Ingrid home so early in her life? Why has this child been left motherless? I don't know the answers to these questions, but we can rest assured God has not made a mistake. He is not punishing us or Ingrid by taking her home. Indeed God has a plan in all this. In Romans 8:28 we read, 'And we know that all things work together for good to them that love God, to them who are the called according to his purpose.' "

Mara watched those around her carefully. "Amens" were sprinkled throughout the minister's words, and heads nodded in agreement. Could it be as he said?

Pastor Hill continued. "Perhaps at some later date we will be able to look back and catch a glimpse of God's plan in all this. Perhaps not."

He opened his Bible and read, " 'Therefore, we are always confident, knowing that, whilst we are at home in the body, we are absent from the Lord: (For we walk by faith, not by sight:) We are confident, I say, and willing rather to be absent from the body, and to be present with the Lord.' " He closed his Bible and surveyed the crowd. "Let us mourn the absence of Ingrid Manning's physical presence, and let us rejoice that she is now present with the Lord."

Then he quoted the Twenty-third Psalm that she had heard at every funeral.

After that, Mara watched as Cade Manning stepped up to the burial spot and sprinkled dust on top of Ingrid's casket. She saw tears on the faces of everyone there as Cade, with his newborn son, knelt by the grave. Then she and the others turned to leave, allowing a husband to grieve in private.

Mara tossed and turned in bed that night. Her mind spun in every direction but always returned to the funeral. She couldn't shake the reality that one day her body would lie stiffly in a box. Where would her soul go? The thought frightened her beyond anything she'd ever experienced. She believed in God, but was that enough? Pastor Hill had talked in church about the free gift of Jesus. But it couldn't be that easy, could it?

She finally fell into an exhausted sleep long after midnight.

The next day, after serving breakfast and cleaning up, she and Beth started working on her dress again. As she made tiny stitches, Mara's thoughts returned to Ingrid's death. How could the church folk be so sure they were going to heaven? She didn't understand what Jesus' death on the cross had to do with going to heaven.

She glanced at Beth and wondered if an eight-year-old child could give her the answers she needed. Well, it wouldn't hurt to try.

"May I ask you a question, Beth?"

Beth shrugged. "Sure."

Mara pushed the needle through the fabric and pulled the

thread. "I don't understand all this about Jesus dying on the cross. What was the purpose in that? How does that get a person to heaven?"

When the words were out, Mara realized she was asking a question a child couldn't possibly understand, much less explain.

"Oh, that's easy. My ma 'splained it like this. If I did something bad, you know, told a fib or stole a licorice stick from the mercantile, I'd deserve a whuping, right?"

Mara nodded.

"Well, this is how it is. God is perfect, and He can't stand sin, so He sent Jesus to take my place, my whuping."

A glimmer of understanding brightened the corners of Mara's heart. "But what about the free gift the minister always talks about?"

"It's hard to 'splain." Her brows crinkled low over her chocolate-colored eyes. "Getting to heaven is free, like a present. But you gotta accept it. If I handed you a box, wrapped all pretty-like, but you didn't reach out and take it, well, you wouldn't have it."

"I see. So I have to accept God's gift of heaven?"

"Sorta." Beth played with her doll's hair. "But God doesn't like sin, so you gotta be clean, and the only way to be clean is to ask Jesus to forgive you."

Everything suddenly seemed clear. She knew what Pastor Hill had been talking about all these weeks. Who would've thought that a child could make things clear?

"Do you wanna be a Christian? 'Cause I know how. Ma helped me do it when I was six."

Yes, yes, she wanted that—very much. She wanted what Beth and Clay had. She wanted the peace Ingrid had. "What do I have to do?"

"If you believe Jesus died for your sins and res'rected, just pray and ask Jesus to forgive you and tell Him you want to live like He wants you to."

"I'd like to do that."

Beth smiled. "Oh, good, Miss Lawton! You can pray out loud or quiet-like—it doesn't matter which way. God hears you."

Mara bowed her head and closed her eyes. "God, I believe about Your sending Jesus to die on the cross. I believe He did it to pay for my sins and that He was resurrected. I want to accept Your free gift. Amen." Mara opened her eyes to see Beth smiling at her. "That's all?"

"Yep, told you it was easy."

Mara couldn't believe how easy it was. She was one of God's children now. A child of the King, as Beth had said weeks ago. The thought put a bounce in her step the whole day.

Clay finished washing up at the pump and walked into the house. The wonderful aroma of pot roast reached him, and his stomach growled.

Before he could shut the door, Beth burst through the kitchen door. "Clay, guess what! You'll never guess!"

Clay tousled her hair. He hadn't seen Beth this excited in weeks. "Your doll grew wings and flew away!"

She giggled. "No, Silly!"

"Miss Lawton grew wings and flew away?"

"Clay—! It is about Miss Lawton, though." Her eyes sparkled like the reflection of the sun shimmering on the creek. "She asked Jesus into her heart, and I got to show her how!"

As if summoned, Mara came through the kitchen door, the platter of roast beef in her hands. She stopped short when Beth made her announcement, and he saw a flush spread over her cheeks.

Could it be true? He glanced from Beth to Mara. "Mara?"

Her lids lowered, and she set the plate on the table as if to cover her embarrassment. "It's true."

She turned and looked at him. With her eyes she asked for his opinion and approval.

He was quick to respond. "That's great, really great." And it was for more reasons than she knew. Not only was she now a child of God, she was no longer off-limits to him. He felt like kicking up his heels and yelling, "Yeehahh!"

Whoa, Clay! Slow down. Just because she's a Christian now doesn't mean you can barge right in and claim her.

True, she'd been pretty open about her feelings. That in itself amazed him—that of all the men in Cedar Springs, she would want him.

Suddenly he noticed that Mara and Beth had taken their seats. He sat down quickly, and they joined hands.

With a contented smile relaxing his face he prayed, "Father, we thank You for this food, for the hands that prepared it." He paused, wondering if he should say what was on his mind. "And, Lord, thank You for showing Yourself to Mara. May You use her for Your purposes, in Jesus' name, amen." He squeezed Mara's hand.

Her eyes opened wide as her gaze met his. Of course. She hadn't any way of knowing what her decision meant to him. To them. He had never told her what had held him back.

He winked, and Mara lowered her gaze.

"What are we waiting on?" Beth asked, her gaze swinging back and forth between her brother and Mara.

Clay reached out for a slice of pot roast. "Not a thing, Beth—not a thing."

❧

During the next week Mara asked Clay and Beth many questions. She was already growing in her faith and had learned so much in only seven days. She had tried to explain to her parents what had happened in her life, but they didn't understand.

Mara noticed a change in Clay's behavior too. Though they hadn't been alone since the night he helped her saddle a horse, she saw something new in his eyes. It was only one week before Clay's aunt Martha would come home, and Mara dreaded the end of her time here on the Stedman ranch. She would miss spending her days with Beth. But she wouldn't miss the stubborn cookstove or the privy!

When Mara stood to clear the table one night, Clay put his napkin on his plate.

"Mara, may I speak with you?"

Mara blinked. She started to sit back down, but Clay glanced uneasily at Beth.

"I mean alone."

"Oh." She tried to read his eyes but couldn't. "Of course, let me just finish up here—"

"Beth, why don't you take care of cleaning up tonight?"

She made a face. "All right."

Clay stood, and Mara followed him to the door. He allowed her to pass through first.

What was going on? Was he displeased with something she had done? Her meals had improved, or so she thought. She had even figured out how to make decent coffee.

Clay closed the door and turned toward her. He walked to the rail and stuffed his hands in his pockets.

Mara could stand it no longer. "What is it, Clay? Have I done something wrong?"

He turned. "No, it isn't that at all."

"Then what is it?"

He leaned against the rail and studied her face. "I'm not sure how to say it."

Her heart softened at his uncertainty. The sun's last rays shone on his face, and she longed to reach out and touch it. "Whatever it is, you can tell me."

He smiled, and her legs grew weak. How would she manage without seeing him every day?

"Remember when we first met?"

Though his gaze was warm, Mara cringed at the words. She remembered all too well, but she would rather forget.

"I saw you at the dance and watched you from across the barn."

Why was he talking about this? Didn't he know she had changed?

"I was determined as a mule you wouldn't sink your claws into me."

He smiled as if the memory was a fond one, but it wasn't

fond for her at all.

"You reminded me of someone I wanted to forget—someone I was promised to."

"You were engaged?" Just the thought cut off her breath.

"I fell fast and hard for her. Victoria was her name. She was wealthy and comely like you."

Why was he telling her this? Didn't he know it hurt her?

"Little did I know she was using me to make another man jealous—someone who could support her expensive lifestyle. As soon as she had him, she dropped me cold."

Though it hurt to think of him with another, her heart ached at the thought of his pain.

"I thought you were just like her." He leaned forward and took her hand.

Her breath ceased as hope blossomed in her heart.

"Since you've come here, you've changed."

She nodded. Her hand grew damp in his.

"It's as if you had to lose all you had depended on before you could see the woman beneath it all."

Yes. That's exactly what it was.

"I think God had a part in all that."

"Yes, me too."

"He used it to draw you closer to Him."

"I never thought I'd be grateful for everything that's happened in the past few months, but I am now."

"I've come to care deeply for you, you know."

Her heart danced, even while her mouth went dry. She searched his eyes, afraid to hope.

"I wasn't free to act on my feelings until a week ago."

Confusion swirled in her head. She couldn't seem to put two thoughts together.

"You're a believer now. We share a common faith, and that means everything to me." He pulled her closer.

She took in his words and understood. He cared for her. He wanted—

"So many times I wanted to kiss you," he whispered.

He touched her face, and she grew dizzy at the joy. He

drew closer. He was going to kiss her if she didn't faint first.

His lips settled on hers, tentative, testing. Every thought evaporated; every sound hushed. All that existed in that moment were she and Clay. His touch brought sweet ecstasy. This was the way it was meant to be.

He pulled back, and she felt as if half of her had been torn away. She opened her eyes and nearly passed out at his expression.

"Will you go to the harvest social with me?" he whispered.

"Yes." Her heart sang. She would be leaving in a week, but he wanted to court her.

As they said good-bye, Mara was in a daze. He hadn't said the words, but he loved her. She could see it in his eyes. He had held nothing back tonight.

Mara wasn't sure how she reached home. When she arrived there, she realized she didn't remember anything at all. Her mind was still in a daze when she walked through the front door.

"Mara," her mother said when she came through the door, "I'd like a word with you, please."

"What is it, Mother?" Mara followed her into the parlor where her father sat smoking a cigar.

"Have a seat," her mother said.

Mara sank onto the davenport, but her mother remained standing.

"I was at the mercantile today and overheard the most distressing news." She began pacing and mumbling. "The nerve of him—going to church—deceiving us all—"

"Mother, what's this about?"

"That Clay Stedman, that's what! He's an Indian, a savage! Not fit for decent company. He slithered his way into our town, subjected my own daughter to who knows what, and I'll not have it!"

Mara's stomach churned. She had found out; it was bound to happen. But—

"Has he harmed you in any way, Darling?" She sat beside Mara and took her hand. "Touched you? You must tell me the truth."

Anger stirred in the depths of her soul. How could her mother think such things? He would never harm her or anyone else. "Of course not, Mother—don't be ridiculous."

Mrs. Lawton drew back.

"He's just a man, like any other, and—"

"You knew!" Her mother's eyes widened. "You've been going to his house every day for months, and you knew? Haven't you any thought for what people think? For your own reputation?" She reached for her fan and began fluttering it before her face.

Mara was ashamed of her mother's behavior. She acted as if being an Indian was a crime, as if Clay were human garbage. It hurt and angered her deeply. She felt her heart pounding in her ears.

"People will talk," her mother said. "Everyone will find out he's a savage, and your name will be associated with his!"

"Now, Letitia, no real harm has been—"

"He's been alone with our child every day for weeks!"

Disgust rose from the depths of her heart. "I'm no child, Mother, and Clay is no savage!"

"Clay! Since when did you come to be on a first-name basis, young lady?"

Mara knew her mother's sister had been killed by Indians, but was that legitimate cause for her prejudice? It would be like thinking all white men were murderers if only one had committed the crime.

Suddenly she knew what she had to do. Her mother would be appalled, but she wouldn't hide her feelings.

"Mother." She gave her father a beseeching look. "Father, I'm afraid I have more news that might come as a shock."

Her mother's hand fluttered faster. "Oh, my—"

"Clay and I—what I mean to say is, well, we have feelings for each other."

The fan fell to the floor. Her mother's face went from flushed to pasty white in a matter of moments. She swayed. "Oh dear—!"

Her father jumped up from his chair and ran to support his

wife's weight. She wavered, and her eyes glazed.

Mara touched her mother's arm and made eye contact. "Mother."

She didn't respond.

"Letitia, snap out of it."

Her mother blinked and seemed to gather her faculties. "Oh, no! No, it won't happen. I simply will not allow it!"

"Mother, you can't disallow feelings. I needn't have your permission to care for someone. It's something that can't be helped!"

"Be that as it may, young woman—you will not continue with this relationship! I forbid it!" Her father retrieved the fan, and her mother started fluttering again, this time with sharp, angry jerks. "What has this family come to?" She brought her hand to her chest as if her heart were pained. Her eyes spouted tears. "We've lost our money, we've lost our standing, and now we'll be associated with the lowest of the low, the scourge of our nation, absolute savages. Why, you wouldn't be able to turn your head, Mara, without wondering if the heathen was going to take your scalp!"

Mara rose with a sharp breath. How dare she categorize Clay that way! "You are wrong, Mother! You know nothing of Clay, you know nothing of his people, and it's unfair of you to say he's a savage!"

Her mother also stood. "Your own aunt is a tragic example of his kind! Why, they burned the house to the ground with her family in it. If that's not savage, I don't know what is!"

"Clay is a gentle, caring man—a Christian!" Her head felt light, and her body trembled.

"Ha! His people worship Satan! They work voodoo and cast spells and conjure spirits!"

"You have no idea what—"

"Ladies—ladies." Mr. Lawton stepped between his wife and his daughter, holding out his hands. "Shush!"

His command echoed in the sudden silence of the room. Mara's mother took the opportunity to assert herself.

"He may not court you, and that's final!"

Mara's stomach was churning. Her mother could not stop the feelings she felt for Clay. Nor could Mara imagine denying the relationship a chance to develop now that it had finally begun. "Mother, I'm a grown woman. You haven't the—"

"You are my daughter, you live under my roof, and you eat my food. I have every right to forbid this relationship, and I do! There will be no arguing that point! And you will stop going to his house every day. Enough damage has been done."

How could her mother do it? She had finally found someone to care for—someone who cared about her. Not because of her beauty but in spite of it. And she was committed to continue her work until his aunt returned. She took up the easier of the two demands. "I have to finish my work there. Clay's aunt returns in a week, and there's no one to watch Beth or cook or clean."

Her mother appeared to be getting control of her temper. She breathed deeply and cast a glance at her husband. "I don't think that's a good idea."

"Now, Letitia, it's only a week. She's been over there every day for three months—"

"What will people think?" her mother muttered.

"If people are going to get their hackles up over this, the damage is already done. What can one more week matter?"

"Please, Mother." She was willing to plead and beg. She would do the same for Clay's right to call.

Her mother snapped her fan closed, her color now closer to its usual shade. "All right—I'll allow it. But after that it stops—do you hear me? I don't want that man to come calling, and if he does, I'll chase him out of here with a shotgun myself!"

Mara decided to choose her battles. She could fight this one later. "Yes, Mother."

Her mother turned and walked across the room. At the door she stopped and looked back. "One week, Mara, and not one day more."

seventeen

Mara had been awake well into the night, and this morning she saw and felt the results. Even coffee did little to revive her energy. Seeing Clay had reinforced what she had decided long after the moon had ascended high in the sky. Regardless of what her mother thought, she would continue to see Clay. It was her mother who was wrong. Mara would not allow her mother's prejudice to ruin things with Clay.

As she worked on her gown for the harvest social, she took special care, now that Clay would be her escort. The thought put a smile on her face. This year would be so different from other years. She would not seek to dance with as many partners as she could. She was interested in only one partner, and she didn't care if everyone in the town approved of him or not.

She held up the section she had just finished. The sleeve now ended in a long, lacy frill of ivory. Not as elegant as her imported gowns, but it would do very nicely.

Only one week left at the Stedman ranch. She wondered if one day she would return as Clay's bride. Her face grew warm at the thought. They had not even had their first outing, and already she had him at the altar. But he had kissed her—and, oh my, how his touch made her dizzy. Her heart was pounding even at the thought.

After she finished the other sleeve, she called Beth in and fixed a simple lunch. The afternoon wore on, and Mara's thoughts kept returning to her mother's words the night before. She would have to tell Clay. There was really no way around it. When he eventually called on her, he would doubtless find out how her mother felt. Letitia Lawton would never say to his face what the matter really was. Despite what she had said about chasing Clay off with a gun, she wouldn't be that direct. Instead she would turn a cold shoulder. She would snub him until he stopped coming around.

Mara could hardly bear the thought of her own mother hurting the man she loved. She was going to have to tell Clay, but how would she? How would she tell him her parents disapproved of him because he was born to an Indian mother? Hadn't Mara herself been born to a drunk? How was that any different?

When supper was served and the three sat around the table, Mara glanced at Beth. She was a pleasant child, sweet and obedient. How could anyone think she was a savage? She looked at Clay with his smiling eyes and gentle hands. He would never hurt anyone the way her mother had hurt her the night before. Tonight she would have to hurt him the same way. It made her heart ache to think of causing him pain, but if she didn't tell him, he would find out in a much worse way.

If Clay noticed her silence, he didn't say anything. After the supper dishes were washed, Clay accompanied her out to the porch. Beth, seeming to sense they wanted to be alone, went to her room with her doll.

Clay shut the door behind him as Mara leaned against the porch railing. She watched him approach, and a smile played on her lips. He was everything she'd ever wanted in a man and more. Strong, kind, sincere. And stubborn. She couldn't forget that. Her smile widened.

"What're you smiling about?" He smiled in response.

"Maybe you don't want to know," she teased.

"On the contrary, I'm most curious."

Mara raised her chin. She had to in order to look him in the eyes. She arched her brows. "I was thinking, Mr. Stedman, how very stubborn you are."

"And you think that's funny?"

"Mostly it's frustrating."

He laughed before his expression became serious. The two exchanged a look that left Mara's legs wobbly.

"Beth tells me you're making a dress for the social."

"I am."

"I can't wait to see you in it."

"You don't even know what it looks like."

"It could be a burlap bag, and you'd still look beautiful."

She giggled at the thought. My, wouldn't the town be surprised if she appeared attired that way? Clay chuckled with her.

"I can't believe you'll be gone in less than a week," Clay said.

She couldn't believe it herself. She had grown used to seeing him every day. It was enough to spoil a girl. "Have you heard from your aunt?"

"A letter came a week ago. She's still planning to come back on Saturday."

"You'll probably be glad to see the back of me when you taste her fine cooking again."

"You have a good point there, Fancy Pants."

She swatted his arm, but she knew her eyes conveyed her humor. He made her laugh; he made her feel; he made her complete.

She looked away, breaking the moment. How was she to tell him about her mother? She could scarcely bear to see the smile disappear from his eyes. Her gaze swung downward to the porch planks she had swept that afternoon. *God, show me the way to tell him. I don't know what to—*

"What is it?" He tilted her chin up until her eyes met his.

What now? She didn't want to say it, nor could she form the words on her lips. She was ashamed of her mother and ashamed that she herself had treated others in the same way.

"What?"

The touch of his hand made her feel cherished. Her gaze met his. "I—I have something I need to tell you. But I don't know how to say it."

His eyes searched hers. "Just say it plain, Mara. What is it?"

She turned away. She couldn't bear to see his face when she said it. "My mother found out you're half Indian, and she—" The words jammed in her throat. He had undoubtedly faced prejudice before. There was no reason to tell him why her mother felt the way she did, to tell him about her aunt. But she was ashamed that her own mother—

"She disapproves."

His voice was strained, but she still didn't turn around. "I'm afraid so."

Around them the trees rustled in the wind, the only noise that broke their silence. Finally he reached out and turned her toward him. "And you? How do you feel about it?"

She looked at him then. He stood stiffly, his eyes guarded. "Oh, Clay, you know I don't care about that!" All the conviction she felt was surely shining in her eyes. "I've known for weeks, and has my behavior given you cause to question this?"

Gradually the shadows fell from his eyes. He gave a tiny smile. "No." His chest expanded with a deep breath then fell with the exhale. "I'm sorry. I had no reason to ask that."

"Prejudice is nothing new to you, I'm sure."

"Still, I know better than to think that you—"

"Hush," she said, laying a finger over his lips. "I know you meant nothing by it." Her hand fell away.

"Do your parents know how we—?" He didn't have to finish the sentence.

"I told them."

His gaze probed hers. "Have they forbidden you to see me?"

She tried to smile but failed. "They have."

A crease formed between his brows. His eyes clouded, but she saw the question in them.

She pulled herself straight and tall. "I'm not going to listen. She's wrong—we both know that."

"She's your mother—"

"But she's wrong."

"I know, Mara, but how can we see one another if your parents forbid it?"

Surely he wouldn't give in to her parents' wishes. The thought of losing him was too much for her heart to grasp. "I'm a grown woman, Clay, and am perfectly capable of choosing my own beau."

He smiled then, and his eyes lit with humor. "Is that what I am?"

A flush spread across her face. Was it too early to call him her beau? They hadn't even had their first outing, but she felt she knew him better than all the other suitors she'd had.

"I'm teasing," he said soberly and lowered his voice to a whisper. "I'd be proud to call you mine."

He was so near that his breath brushed her cheeks. Her heart seemed to skip a beat, and her legs grew weak. She was almost dizzy with pleasure at his words. She wanted him to kiss her again—wanted it so badly that she nearly leaned forward and initiated it herself.

He looked away. "I need time to think about it. To figure out what's right."

"But—" She couldn't beg.

"Maybe I can change your mother's mind, if she got to know me—"

She couldn't give him false hopes about that. She shook her head. It was enough.

"She's all right with you coming here the rest of the week?"

"I didn't give her much choice."

He gave a little laugh. "Now there's the Fancy Pants I know and—" The smile disappeared from his face.

Love. He'd been about to say it—she knew he had. But he choked off the word, leaving her hungry for it. An awkward silence gathered around them.

He cleared his throat. "Well, I'll go hitch up your team."

She nodded and, as he walked away, wondered if she would ever hear the words she longed for.

❧

Mara spent the rest of the week worrying, although she enjoyed her last days with Beth and was pleased with the girl's improvement in manners. But something was wrong with Clay. He avoided spending time alone with her. In the mornings they were always in the company of his ranch hands, and in the evenings Beth was always present. Mara had even tried to coax him out on the porch. She desperately wanted to know what he was thinking. But he always hitched up her rig and returned to the house before she finished cleaning up. The week had started with worry, but now it had spiraled into dread. She had the horrible suspicion he was going to abide by her mother's wishes, and the thought made her anxious.

Finally Friday arrived, the last day before Aunt Martha's return. She and Beth spent the day cleaning the house until it sparkled and baking a special cake to celebrate Martha's return. But celebrating was the last thing Mara wanted to do. She was sure tonight Clay was going to speak with her, and she was equally sure he was going to end their relationship before it even began.

Mara fixed a special supper that night: fried chicken with all the fixings. And this time her chicken was crisp to perfection. When she brought the platter to the table, Beth and Clay marveled at the array of food. Despite her worry, Mara felt a glimmer of pride as she surveyed the delicious-looking food. She had come a long way. She could cook, sew, clean, do laundry, feed hogs, gather eggs—why, she had learned more in the past three months than she had in her entire life!

During the prayer Mara savored the feeling of Clay's hand wrapped big and strong around hers. Would it be the last time they touched in such a way? *Oh, Lord, let it not be so!*

Conversation was sparse during the meal, though Mara noticed Beth did her very best to display proper table manners. When they were in the kitchen putting away the food, Mara laid her hand on Beth's shoulder.

"You have been an excellent pupil, Beth Stedman. You could dine with the queen and do me proud."

Beth smiled. "Thank you." Then her smile faded, and her face grew sad.

"Why, whatever's the matter?" Mara leaned down to the little girl's eye level.

"I'm gonna miss you, Miss Lawton!" She threw herself at Mara, wrapping her arms around her waist.

Mara's heart softened. Her eyes burned with unshed tears. She would miss Beth too, but she tried not to think about it now that the parting was almost here.

"Now, now, shush, Darling," she whispered. "I'm only a short walk away. You can come and visit me anytime." She gave the reassurance as much for herself as for Beth.

Beth looked up at her, the tears lingering on her lashes then spilling onto her cheeks. "Really—you mean it?"

Mara laughed. "Of course I do. How else am I going to learn how to make shirts and trousers for my father?"

Beth choked out a laugh. "I don't even know how to do that."

"Then we'll learn together, yes?" Mara asked. "Now dry up those tears and give me a hand with the dishes, all right?"

Beth was cheerful after that, but inside Mara a knot of fear tightened. One way or another she must find out where Clay stood before she left. She would not be put off tonight.

As it turned out, she didn't need to assert herself. Before she finished with the dishes, he peeked his head through the kitchen door.

"Mara, may I have a word with you when you're finished? On the porch?"

His tone was casual, but she saw the tension in his face. "Of course, I'll be right out."

After he left, Beth took the cup Mara was washing. "You go on. I'll finish up here."

Mara smiled at her. "Why, thank you, Beth." Mara hung up her apron and made her way to the front door. Her legs trembled, and her stomach felt as though the chicken supper had congealed in a queasy lump. *Please, God, don't take him away from me.*

She stepped through the door to see Clay half-sitting on the porch rail. The days were growing shorter, and the sun was slipping over the horizon behind Clay. The bright swashes of pink and periwinkle silhouetted his figure.

She moved to his side where she could read his face. Then

she wished she hadn't. It was there, written in his eyes, in his sad smile.

"I've been doing a lot of thinking and praying this week," Clay said.

She looked away. She could smell the soap on his skin. The soap she'd made herself.

"You're a Christian now, Mara, and I hope you can understand what I'm about to say."

Mara felt like holding her hands over her ears and humming as she had once seen a child do. Only the reality that it wouldn't change matters kept her from it.

"The Bible is clear on its expectations of children—even grown ones. Your mother doesn't want me courting you, and I think we have to respect that."

Though she fully expected the words, they still sent an ache deep in her bones. She wanted to say something. She wanted to convince him he was wrong. "How can you be willing to give in so easily?" Her voice was husky. "My mother's wrong to feel the way she does, and you know it."

He nodded. "That doesn't change things. Until your parents are willing to give us their blessings, we—"

"That's not going to happen!" Desperation set in. He seemed so sure, so resolute, so—stubborn.

"Be that as it may, we have to respect their wishes."

"They're my parents! If I'm willing to thwart their authority, you should be willing too." She fought the urge to stamp her foot.

His jaw flinched. "Don't make this difficult, Mara."

She grabbed his arm and looked at him, her heart in her eyes. "Please, Clay, let's give it a chance. They don't even have to know—"

He looked away, and she saw something flicker in his eyes. All at once it hit her. Perhaps he no longer wanted to court her. Perhaps he was only using her parents as an excuse. The anger drained away, and something much worse took its place. Was she making a fool of herself? Pleading with him for something he didn't want. She felt heat rush to her face. Maybe the changes in her life weren't enough. Maybe he still thought she was spoiled and frivolous. Her eyes began to sting, and she turned away. She had no intention of crying, but just in case she would not let him see it.

"Try to understand," Clay said. "I need to do what's right here. So do you."

"Stop it, Clay!" She'd had enough of his excuses. "Tell me the truth—I can accept it!"

Silence intruded, nudging its way between the two of them and expanding until it swallowed them both. She wished she could see his face, read his thoughts. Just when she thought she might faint, she felt his hands on her shoulders, turning her around.

◆

Clay replayed Mara's words in his head. *"Tell me the truth—I can take it."* He hadn't a clue what she was getting at. Why couldn't womenfolk speak plain? He studied her face, wishing she would look at him. "Mara." He tilted her chin until her gaze met his. What was in those beautiful blue eyes, as clouded as a stormy sky? "What are you saying?"

Her eyes flashed. "I don't think my parents have anything to do with your decision. I think you've changed your mind, and they are a convenient excuse."

He frowned. "What?"

"If you don't want to court me, say it!" Her chin edged up, and he saw a bit of the spunkiness he liked so well.

"That's not true!" he said. He took hold of her shoulders and shook her gently. "I want more than anything to. This has been a hard decision—I've been fighting with it all week."

"You've been avoiding me all week."

He smiled inwardly at the pout on her face. He wanted to take her in his arms and show her how much he wanted to court her.

"It was the only way to keep my head clear. I need to base my decision on what's right—not on what I want."

Her eyes softened. "Truly?"

"I would never lie to you." His hand reached up and cupped her cheek. Her skin felt so soft, and the way she leaned into his hand made him yearn for her. When she closed her eyes and placed a kiss on his palm, he had to pull away.

The hurt in her eyes tormented him.

"I can't stand the thought of not seeing you." Tears pooled in her eyes but didn't spill over the rim of lashes.

"We'll still see one another," he whispered.

"It will be different."

It will be awful—that's what it'll be, he thought. Seeing one another but being unable to talk and laugh together, for doing so would only bring them more pain.

The horses at the side of the house whinnied impatiently.

"I don't want to say good-bye."

He looked at her then, soaking up every detail about her. The dark blue flecks in her eyes, the creamy skin, the faint freckles on her nose. *Why, Lord? I thought she was the one for me. I want her so much.*

But not enough to disobey God's commands. He was ashamed at how close he had come to giving in the past few days.

"Let's not then."

Her gaze fell to the ground, and she stepped around him and walked down the porch steps. At the bottom she turned, and his traitorous heart felt a spring of hope.

"Tell Beth I said good-bye."

Disappointment weighed him down. He nodded his head once, not wanting to risk speaking around the lump in his throat. He watched her climb onto the wagon seat and flick the reins. She held her back stiff, her head straight. He willed her to look at him one more time, but she didn't. She rode away a different Mara than she had come, and this Mara took his heart with her.

eighteen

The next morning Mara awoke before dawn. After dressing, she sat on the window seat, ignoring the rumbling in her stomach. The stagecoach would be arriving soon, and she had a prime seat to view its stop. She felt pitiable, sitting there waiting for a glimpse of Clay. A part of her hoped his aunt had been detained and that they would need her for another day or two. Not that it would change anything. She knew from Clay's resolution the night before that his mind would not be changed.

Her mother had been standoffish all week, and Mara knew it was because she'd disapproved of Mara's working this last week at the Stedmans'. Last night she had been her usual self, but it had been Mara who was out-of-sorts. Her mother was getting her own way, but Mara was the one suffering now.

She tried to imagine her life without Clay, but she couldn't. She couldn't go back to her old ways. She was a Christian now and knew that her flirtatious ways had hurt people. Besides that, she hadn't the desire to toy with other men now. What used to be an amusing sport seemed now an empty, futile game.

I'm new to all this, Jesus. Help me understand. Help me be strong. If You don't mean for Clay and me to be together, please take these feelings away.

A clattering sound drew Mara's attention, and she looked down onto the dawn-tinted street. Her heart caught in her throat. Clay. She dropped the lacy curtain, knowing she could still see through it but not wanting him to see her.

But, oh, the sight of him sent blood surging through her limbs and made her breathing shallow. How could his presence affect her so?

The wagon drew to a halt at the Coopers' boardinghouse. She had to stretch her neck to see him step off the wagon and help Beth down. He wore his nice trousers and a red and black plaid shirt she had darned a few weeks ago. She could almost feel its worn softness now.

Clay and Beth stepped up on the porch of the boarding-house, and he leaned against the pillar. *How will I bear seeing him at church every week, knowing he will never be mine? Oh, Clay, how I love you.*

As if her message had been borne through the air, he turned. Her heart skittered to a halt. The breath froze in her lungs. He looked right at her window, right at her. She wished he were nearer so she could read his eyes. Could he see her beyond the lacy veil? She wanted to tear it open and press her hand to the window, but she couldn't move. Couldn't think. And then he turned away.

She felt as if her heart had collapsed under a crushing weight. He was so near, yet so far. Did it tear at him too? Did he ache as she did?

She turned away from the window. Why was she torturing herself so? She glanced around her room, and her gaze fell upon her new dress hanging from a hook beside her armoire. She had worked so hard on it, and it had turned out nicely. She had thought she would wear it when she and Clay attended the harvest social together—had thought about it with every stitch and knot. Now she would attend alone, and the beauty of the dress would be wasted.

A sound drew her attention to the street below her window. She saw the stage round the corner and draw to a halt at the boardinghouse. Moments later Mrs. Stedman clambered down the steps. Mara watched her hug Beth then Clay. They smiled and laughed while the driver fetched her bags; then the coach was gone, and Clay was loading the wagon. She watched him help his aunt and sister onto the wagon seat and climb up himself. With the flick of the reins he drove away without another look, leaving Mara feeling more alone than she'd ever felt before.

ఎ

Mara muddled through the next weeks, and in an effort to pass time she took over most of the household chores. She had never realized before how much work Sadie had been responsible for. But keeping her hands busy didn't keep her mind from thoughts of Clay. She both dreaded and looked forward to Sundays when she would see him again. How her heart could feel at such odds was a mystery to her. It wasn't as if they talked at church. They barely even looked at one other, for to do so was sweet agony. Her one consolation was that the few times their eyes met, she read the ache in his eyes. He missed her too, and though it didn't change things, it helped to know her feelings were returned.

She was still not on the best of terms with her mother. Not that she was exacting revenge by being withdrawn, but she had trouble manufacturing feelings of amiability when this separation was her mother's fault. It further annoyed her that her mother seemed content to laze about the house doing nothing while Mara cooked, cleaned, and did almost every other household chore.

When the day of the harvest social arrived, Mara's heart churned. Her new dress was loose in the waist, confirming Mara's suspicion that she had lost weight. She wondered what would happen tonight. Since her parents were not attending, she had hopes that Clay would dance with her, if only once. The thought of being in his arms again made her head spin. Would she have to watch Clay dance with other women? Her stomach knotted at the thought.

Though she had become adept at styling her hair, she chose to wear it the way Clay preferred, pulled back on the sides and hanging straight down her back.

The social was being held at the Farnsworths' farm, a short walk away, where the huge new barn lent itself to big crowds. As she neared it, she saw light spilling out through the doors and windows. The strains of fiddle music floated out, and Mara could feel the celebratory spirit of the farmers whose harvest was safely in. The smell of new lumber still lingered in the air.

She stopped as she neared the doors, her heart racing in her chest. For a moment she considered leaving. Why was she exposing herself to the disappointment she would feel if Clay didn't come, to the agony if he did? It was futile unless she could convince him to change his mind. And she didn't see much hope there.

She commanded her feet to move, and she advanced on shaky legs. When she reached the opened door, she let her gaze wander around the crowd. When her gaze lit on Clay, every muscle stilled in her body. He was talking to Luke and Caleb Reiley and had not spotted her yet. She was transported back to that day in the spring when she had seen him for the first time. He was every bit as handsome to her now as he was then, but now she possessed a solid knowledge of him as a person. She no longer saw him as sport, but as the man who held her heart.

He turned and saw her then. Her knees nearly buckled. A sad grin tugged at the corner of his lips, and he gave a small wave. Her own fingers fluttered in response. She was torn at what to do next but was saved from the decision by Sara McClain.

"You look beautiful, Mara." Sara hugged her.

Mara was momentarily stunned. She had never been hugged by another woman, save her own mother and Sadie. She decided she liked a friend's hug. "Thank you." They pulled apart, and Mara noticed the intricate stitching on the bodice of Sara's gown. That led to a long conversation on sewing.

Even while they talked, Mara kept glancing at Clay, but he wasn't looking at her. Daniel and several others approached her, asking to dance, but Mara politely turned them down.

Beth came over awhile later. "Miss Lawton!" She threw her arms around Mara in a big hug.

"I've missed you, Darling. Have you been practicing your good manners?"

"Yes, Ma'am. Aunt Martha is plum tickled about it."

Beth chatted about the new school year with her and Sara

and mentioned that Clay would be leaving soon for roundup. Mara wondered how long he would be gone. Beth said a whole passel of men would be going to round up the cattle before the cold set in.

When a slow tune began, Sara's husband spirited her to the dance floor. Mara turned to look at Clay. Both Luke and Caleb escorted their wives to the floor, leaving Clay alone.

He turned to look at her, and her feet began the walk toward him. She walked around bales of hay and clusters of friends, her gaze fastened on Clay. He watched her approach, and his torso straightened. He glanced around, and Mara knew he was searching for her mother.

"She's not here," Mara said over the music.

His gaze returned to her face, and she watched him touch each feature like a caress. "We still shouldn't—"

His words cut off, though she knew what he was going to say. "Just one dance."

His jaw worked, and he looked away.

"Please, Clay, I've missed you so."

When he remained silent, she reached out and took his hand. He looked at her then, and she wondered if her heart were in her eyes.

He led her a few steps away and turned, keeping her one hand in his and putting the other at her waist.

Her heart soared at his touch. They moved slowly, keeping a respectable distance between them. She wanted to ask him how he'd been, how Beth was doing. She wanted to ask if he'd missed her, but her throat closed up.

He looked everywhere but at her, and she felt the tension in his arms, in the way he held her. She wished the song would go on forever. At least he'd agreed to the dance.

"Thank you," she said.

He glanced at her, his eyes laced with pain. "This is madness," he whispered.

She didn't have to ask what he meant. If only he would change his mind. They could see one another without her parents' knowledge. She smothered the twinge of guilt. "We could meet somewhere—"

He looked away. "It would be wrong."

"I'm a grown woman."

His gaze returned to her, pleading. "Don't make it any harder than it already is."

She wanted to drown in his eyes, melt into him, and never be separated. Perhaps he did not feel as strongly as she. The thought brought a surge of pain. But when she studied him, studied his eyes, she knew it was not so.

The music ended, and the group applauded the players. Clay pulled away, and she released him, suddenly feeling very empty.

"I need to get home," he said.

He was leaving because of her, and they both knew it. Her throat clogged with tears. "Good-bye."

With one last look he turned and left, collecting Beth on the way.

Later that night, as she lay in bed, Mara finally let the tears fall. Tonight had only given her a taste of what she was missing. It was like being on the brink of paradise and being denied entrance. Why couldn't her mother accept him?

She wiped her face with her imported coverlet. She had to think of a way to be with him again. He wouldn't meet with her secretly, so she would have to set it up herself somehow. But, she remembered, he was going to be rounding up cattle and would be gone for days.

Beth's words echoed in her mind. A whole passel of men would go with him.

An idea began to grow. Before Mara went to sleep, she knew precisely what she would do, and the smile that formed on her face remained until she was sound asleep.

nineteen

Three days later Mara slipped out of the house before dawn and saddled up one of her father's horses. The cowboy duds she'd borrowed from Daniel Parnell's fourteen-year-old brother felt strange on her. If her mother saw her dressed as she was she'd have a fit of apoplexy! She felt a moment of guilt at the thought. She had told her parents she was taking the stage to Wichita to visit Sadie for a couple of weeks. Though her mother had complained about having to do all the chores, she eventually relented, knowing how Mara had missed their cook. By the time her parents awoke, they would assume she was on her way to Wichita. A bit of doubt wormed through her, but she pressed it firmly away. It was her parents who were wrong. Why should she feel guilty?

Since several of the local ranchers were participating in the roundup, Mara knew she could blend in with the many cowpokes. She only hoped she could perform her job well enough to fool them until they were far enough away that Clay wouldn't send her home.

She would have nearly two weeks with Clay, perhaps enough time to convince him to thwart her parents' authority. When she reached the Stedman ranch, there was already a buzz of activity. Cowboys were waiting astride their saddled horses, talking and laughing in the early morning light.

No one spoke to her when she rode up, and when Clay walked past, she ducked her head, letting the brim of the hat hide her face. She was much smaller than the others, but she hoped they would assume she was an adolescent.

Before long they were off, and Mara smiled to herself. This was going to be easier than she thought. Clay was riding at the front of the group some fifty men ahead of her. When they reached the valley, they met up with the men from the other ranches. The owners caught up with Clay and rode alongside him. Mara watched the sun rise from her saddle, content and eager to put some miles behind her.

It didn't take long to figure out that riding at the back had its disadvantages. The dirt stirred up by the cowpokes and cattle was heavy and thick, and she had neglected to bring a handkerchief like the ones she saw the others wearing around their noses and mouths. It felt as if her mouth and lungs were coated with dust.

As the day wore on, she learned what to do from watching the others. They were gathering any cattle they found and driving them into a herd. They looked behind every boulder, thicket, and tree. Several times one of the leaders would motion her off to look behind some tree, and she banged on a tin can to scare the cow out into the open as she'd seen the others do. She was relieved she hadn't had to use her rope yet. The others whipped it through the air with the ease of someone who had done it all their lives. Mara had never tried to rope anything.

It was nigh on noon when they stopped for a meal. Mara followed the others as they gathered around the chuck wagon. She was famished, and her backside was more than a little sore.

By the time she had a plate of food, she didn't care that it was only beef jerky or that the potatoes had no salt or spice. A boy of about fifteen, Matthew, had a seat beside her and talked to her while they ate. She tried to lower her voice to sound masculine, and it must have worked.

After their noon meal the day wore on. The job was hard, and being in a saddle all day had made her whole back ache. She would be doubly sore tomorrow.

Late in the afternoon, a leader named Finigan sent her toward some boulders and thickets to check for cattle. Confident she'd nearly made it through the day, Mara rounded the foliage to find a cow stuck in the briar patch. She knew what she was supposed to do: whirl her lariat over her head and send it sailing onto the cow's head. But it was easier said than done. She made four attempts and was about to get off her mount and lead the cow out when her dinner mate trotted up on his horse. Unfortunately she knew he'd had to witness her pathetic attempts at roping.

"Need a hand?"

Mara smiled in relief. "Sure, uh, never could get the hang of this roping."

Matthew twirled the loop and sent it flying straight over the cow's head. When the cow pulled away, the rope went taut, pulling the loop tight around its neck. Seeing he had it under control, Mara nodded her thanks and rode off.

By the time the sun was slipping over the horizon, the group finally stopped for the night. Mara's body ached so much that she didn't know if she could stand upright. How could a body sit all day and wind up so sore? She was bone weary enough to skip supper, but doing so would be suspect. Already Matthew was casting suspicious glances at her. She had managed to avoid Clay so far, and no one else paid her any mind.

When they reached a site near a shallow creek, they all gathered around the chuck wagon. After leading their horses to the creek, some of the men removed tin cups from their saddlebags while others used their hats to scoop water to their mouths. Mara hadn't thought to bring a cup, and she surely couldn't remove her hat and expose the lengths of hair she'd secured to her head. Her mouth tasted of dust and was just as dry. She cupped her hands and drank from the creek, aware that she was drinking from the same source as dozens of horses. She was too thirsty to care.

After she drank, she washed the thick layer of dust from her forearms and face. She only wished she could do something about the filthy clothes she wore. She'd brought another set of clothing, but she wondered when she would be able to sneak off and change. She would have to wait until the others changed, though, in order to fit in. She wrinkled her nose. She could smell them from here, and they didn't seem at all concerned about it.

Supper that night was something called frijoles, which looked and tasted like plain old dried beans. It was accompanied by more biscuits and finished with pudding. Mara didn't have to force herself to eat heartily. Regardless of the bland food, her stomach begged for more.

As the darkness fell, she noticed Matthew across the fire from her. The firelight cast a golden glow on his face, and a frown flickered between his brows. The cool evening air brushed over the hairs on her arms, raising chill bumps along the way. She averted her eyes. He knew something was awry. She had to hide her identity for at least a couple of more days.

As poker games and music broke out, she couldn't keep her focus off Clay. Though most of the men said things that made her face heat up, Clay kept his language fit for a lady's ears.

She spread out her bedroll and lay back on it, resting her head on her saddlebag. The ground felt as hard as wood, and her lumpy bag was no pillow. Regardless, her eyelids closed to the lively harmonica tunes, and then she was oblivious to anything at all.

ò

"Rise and shine! Come a-runnin', boys!"

If the shout hadn't awakened Mara, the ruckus of pots and pans surely would have. She stirred in her bedroll. Oh, how her body ached! She couldn't move without every muscle screaming with pain.

The man closest to her was already up and moving. "Grub pile, Son—up and at 'em."

It took a moment for her to realize she was the son he was speaking to. She sat up gingerly, biting her lip at the pain. The man next to her must have noticed. "Feelin' a bit sore, are you? You needs to get yourself up and moving 'bout."

Mara didn't know if she could even walk. She rubbed her eyes. She felt as if she needed several hours more of sleep, but the hunger that roared in her stomach would only be assuaged if she could make it over to the fire. The smell of fried bacon beckoned her.

She climbed out of her bedroll, standing slowly. The pain took her breath away. And she thought she had been sore after her first days at the Stedman ranch!

She tried to walk without limping and must have succeeded since no one said anything. When she had filled her plate, she found a seat far away from Clay and Matthew.

As she spooned food into her mouth, she realized that even her fingers hurt. How would she make it another day in the saddle? And yet she had to if she wanted Clay to let her stay when she revealed her identity to him.

Already some of the men were finished eating and had begun to saddle up. Her backside protested. The sun was not yet up, and they were prepared to work.

The thought of getting in the saddle again made her want to scream. Her body ached, she was filthy, and she wanted to sleep! The fact that none of the others seemed uncomfortable or unhappy only made her more frustrated.

Putting the saddle up on the horse was an effort that attracted teasing laughs from the cowboys around her. Only her frustration gave her the strength she needed to hoist the saddle on.

She was sent out with others to round up the cattle in the area. She was glad to be doing something familiar but hoped she wouldn't have to use her lariat in front of anyone else. She imitated the men, smacking the backside of wandering cows and hawing with a loud voice.

"You there!" one of the leaders shouted at her. "Bogged cow!" He pointed past her to a cow that was stuck in the mud at the edge of the creek.

Dread set in. She had seen a seasoned cowpoke yesterday trying to get a cow out of mud. Not only had he used his lariat, but he'd worked at it for a long time before succeeding.

She headed toward the cow, hoping no one would notice the

difficulties she was sure to have.

She tied the end of the rope to the horn of her saddle and tried spinning it over her head. She hurled the loop—and missed. Not just the head, but the entire cow. She glanced around, relieved no one had seen.

She tried again—and again—and again. Finally, gritting her teeth, she dismounted and walked over to the cow. Despite her frustration she talked softly so as not to startle the animal. As she neared, the mud sucked at her boots, which were several sizes too big. One of her boots stuck, while her foot came out. She teetered precariously on one foot before grabbing the hide of the cow. The animal flinched away, and she lost her hold.

A moment later she was in the mud. She heard laughter and turned to look. Three cowboys on their mounts had stopped what they were doing to watch.

"Looks like we got ourselves a mail-order cowboy," one of them said.

Another one spit. "As greenhorn as they come. Couldn't hit the broad side of a barn."

Her stomach churned. It was bad enough making a fool of herself, but it was worse worrying they would find out who she was. A woman alone with three rugged men was a recipe for disaster. Mara pulled herself up, the mud clinging to her clothes. Before she could slip the loop over the cow's head, a looped rope came sailing over her head and landed smartly around the cow's neck.

She retrieved her boot and slid her foot inside before they could see how small it was. The mud pulled at her boots as she made her way back to her horse, but she was determined not to lose one. Finally she was on her mount, leaving the other cowboy to handle the cow.

As she rode away, she heard the sniggering and crude comments they exchanged. There were three additional men she needed to avoid.

Their herd grew larger by the hour and became more difficult to keep in line. Mara avoided any bogged cattle, knowing she hadn't the experience to extract them from the mud. She pretended not to see them. She was thankful most of the cows moved along at a whistle or a swat on the hide.

She would tell Clay tomorrow night. She simply couldn't stand this work any longer than that, and surely they would be far enough along that he wouldn't send her home. That thought was the only thing that kept her going all morning.

When she moved in toward the herd, one of the trail bosses glanced at her. "We need a drag rider." He gestured to the back of the herd.

She nodded once. What was a drag rider? She'd learned that her job the day before was called outrider, but that did her little good when she had a different job today.

A young man of about fifteen slowed his mount. "Drag rider?" he asked.

She nodded, wondering what it could be.

"Name's Josh," he stopped his horse as the herd rode past.

She nodded. "Wynn." It was her middle name.

They waited side by side until the entire outfit passed except for a few straggling cows; then he nudged his horse. Mara followed. Well, now she knew a drag rider rode at the end of the herd, but she still didn't know what she should do.

Josh slapped the rumps of the laggards, and Mara followed. It didn't take long to see they were responsible for nudging the slowpokes, mainly calves and ill cattle, with some of them quite scrawny. It was a challenge to move some of them and downright frustrating when some of the beasts had to be nudged every step of the way.

And the dust! She thought she'd caught some dirt yesterday, but it was nothing compared to riding at the tail end of the herd! She didn't even have a canteen of water to wet her mouth. Josh had a handkerchief over his mouth, but she had nothing to filter the dust.

She was not very adept at the job, and she felt Josh's displeasure in the looks he gave her. She was doing her best—couldn't he see that? She thought she was doing very well for someone who was new to this work. Of course, he didn't know that.

Each minute wore on, and she longed for the dinner hour. *Ha. Like we'll have a whole hour to eat.*

It took until noon to gather the cattle, and by then Mara wished she could lay out her bedroll and go back to sleep. She was so weary. By the time she spoke to Clay, she would be too tired to talk.

When at last it was time to stop, she nearly fell out of her saddle, and her legs almost buckled under the weight. Clay passed at that very moment, and she turned quickly away, suddenly having the energy to stand upright.

A river ran nearby, so she took her horse for a drink with the others. Her dry mouth begged for water, and after washing her hands she cupped some water and slurped. Once her thirst was assuaged, she washed the thick layer of grit off her face. Oh, how she longed for clean clothing! The mud she'd fallen into had caked and dried on her trousers. If she were to hang these up and beat the dirt out as she did rugs, it would take an hour.

Sometime later, the cook slopped the food on her plate. She looked down at it. Beans and biscuits. To think she'd looked forward to this. With a mess wagon full of cooking supplies one would think he could come up with something more original. No wonder the poor hands at the Stedman ranch had been so testy when she'd ruined the meals! Their only decent food was what they had at the house.

While eating dinner, Mara found out that after the meal they would sort the cattle by ranch; then each ranch would brand its own calves. The thought made the food in her stomach turn. Her hopes of escaping the work were dashed when all of Clay's men went to work. Some of the men worked by the fire while others began separating the cattle by ranch brand. She joined in the throng, nudging the cattle with the lazy "S" brand into the designated spot.

Once they were separated, each ranch began nudging unbranded cattle out of the herd. The calf's angry mother would follow her offspring, and more than once Mara saw the mother try to knock the cowboys off their horses.

Mara found her first unbranded calf and nudged her from the herd, keeping an eye on the disgruntled mother. Sweat ran down the front and back of her shirt in the afternoon sun. It was a tedious job.

Once she had the calf out of the herd, she slipped the lariat's loop around the calf's head and tightened it. Next she dismounted and tried to drag the fighting calf to the fire. Every time she gained a few feet, the animal would jerk on the rope and pull her back. The fight seemed to go on forever. Her back and arms and legs had about all they could take. She was too weary to stand, much less drag a frightened calf and fend off an angry mother.

When she finally had the calf near the fire, one of the cowboys grabbed it and held it down. Before she could turn away, another cowboy with a red-hot branding iron pressed the hot steel into the calf's side. The calf bawled, his eyes wide and frantic.

The horror of it wrenched her stomach. The stench of burning hair flooded Mara's nose and lungs, and the contents of her stomach threatened to spill. The world began to spin, and everything around her went black, save two tunnels of sight. Her body felt light and dizzy. She swayed.

"Buck up, Boy!"

She heard the words from far away and knew they were directed at her. She fought the darkness, blinking her eyes. She heard laughter and taunting and forced herself to remain upright. Slowly her vision returned, and the dizziness abated. The queasiness remained, and so did the horrible stench.

Several men had stopped their work to gawk. Her gaze fixed on Clay's across the fire. She quickly turned back to her horse. Had he recognized her in that short moment? How could she have swooned, for lands' sake?

"All right, boys, back to work," she heard Clay say.

When she was mounted again, she pulled her hat brim low and glanced at Clay. He was back at work, and a gush of relief flooded her. She looked at the large herd and realized she would have to endure these sounds and smells for quite some time.

Now she ached all over, and she was mortified to boot. Could things get any worse? *This isn't working out so well, God.* She realized for the first time that she'd made her plans without consulting God. Hadn't Beth and Clay told her how she was supposed to let Him lead her? *I'm not doing so well, am I?*

She reached the herd and found another unbranded calf. When the mother eyed her and snorted, Mara almost picked another calf. Moments later she wished she had. She successfully nudged the calf through the herd, but the mother charged at her horse. At the jarring force, her mount skittered sideways. She urged the horse forward after the calf and had just cleared the herd when the mother cow rammed the horse from the side, taking him by surprise. He reared up, and Mara lost her seating.

She grabbed for something, the saddle horn, the saddle, anything that might stop her fall. But the momentum dragged her downward. She slid backward off the horse and sailed through the air. Time moved so slowly that she felt as if she were hanging suspended, but the hard-packed ground relieved her of that theory.

Her backside landed first, and the impact jolted her head so much she felt as if she had slammed it into a tree. Her whole back felt as if it sported a giant bruise. She heard laughter from behind her, which was quickly choked off. She looked around, making sure the mother cow and horse were not about to trample her.

It was then that she noticed the odd silence. The cows continued to moo and snort, but the hawing, the whistling, the talking stopped. She noticed then that all the men were staring. The laughing had stopped, the smiles falling off their faces. Their eyes were wide like those of the bawling calves, and their mouths hung open.

twenty

A moment of confusion washed through Mara's barely functioning mind. Then she saw the hat—her hat—in the dirt a few feet away. She became aware of a long strand of hair blowing across her face. She could feel other strands blowing against her bare neck.

"Mara?" Clay's question held a bushel of disbelief.

Her gaze fastened on him. His open mouth snapped shut, and he crossed his arms over his chest. His nostrils flared. She had seen the same look on his face when Beth had cut up one of his shirts to make a dress for her doll.

She was suddenly very conscious of her improper clothing. It was one thing when they'd thought she was a man, but now—

Clay marched toward her. He would make her go; she could see it clearly. He was not happy to have her here, and a deep part of her soul hurt to know that. This was not working out as she had hoped. She'd been hurt, laughed at. She was sweaty and stinky and achy and dirty. And clearly unwanted.

≈

Clay watched Mara's lip tremble before she caught it with her teeth. So many emotions assaulted him when he realized it was no boy who had fallen from the horse. On the one hand he was angry that she'd deceived them all; on the other he was downright pleased to see her. Only the gawking cowboys had made him realize the woman he loved was dressed improperly in front of a horde of lonely men.

"All right, show's over—get back to work!" His attention never left her. The dirt and dust on her face stopped in a line mid-forehead where her hat had rested. Wonder filled him as he realized what she must've been through the past two days.

142

Mara's eyes brimmed with tears, and Clay suddenly realized she might be hurt.

"You all right?" He was beside her now, but her eyes were turned to the ground.

She nodded.

Clay held his hand out, and she grabbed it. He pulled her to her feet then picked up her hat and set it on her head. Her horse had been rounded up by one of the men.

He took hold of her hand and headed off to the copse of trees a short distance away where they could talk in private. What had possessed her to join the roundup? Dressed as a boy, no less. He glanced back at her as they walked. The clothes hung loosely on her, and she walked awkwardly in the chaps. Her boots flapped with each step, and he knew they must be four sizes too big.

He shook his head. Didn't she know what could have happened to her out there? What if one of the men had discovered she was a woman? She could have been abused in the worst of ways, and he would not have been there to protect her. His blood began to thump in his head as he thought about how careless she'd been. She could've been killed in a stampede, bit by a snake, thrown from a running horse. There was no end to the dangers a man faced on roundups, much less a woman.

He was glad they had made it to the trees, because he wanted answers, and he wanted them now. He let go of her hand and paced from one tree to another, aiming his frustration at her in occasional glances.

She stood quietly, head down, her arms wrapped around each other. At least she had the sense to look contrite.

He started to speak more than once, but the fact that she had put herself at risk on this harebrained scheme riled him until his teeth clenched and ground together.

"I can explain." Her quiet words set him off.

"You'd better explain, Mara Lawton, 'cause I'm just about angry enough to tan your hide." He took his hat off and threw it on the ground. "Do you know what your foolishness could have caused? You could've been seriously hurt, killed, or downright defiled if these men had found out you were a woman at a more opportune time."

Her chin trembled, but he wasn't about to let her off that easily. "And what about your family? Do they know where you are? They're probably worried sick about you and rightly so." He stepped up to her, wanting to shake her shoulders, but refraining from doing so. "So let's have it, Missy. What made you go off on this cock-eyed plan?"

Her eyes met his briefly, the tears puddling on her lower lashes. She covered her face with both hands. "I just wanted to see you—" Her words ended in a wail. Her shoulders shook with sobs.

Clay watched, his emotions bouncing around but settling nowhere. His anger drained away. He felt helpless watching her cry like a baby. Especially after he'd spoken so harshly to her.

"I missed you." He barely heard her over the hawing and the pounding of hooves in the distance. "And this was the only way I could think of to—it's been so hard—my whole body hurts, I have a sunburn, I'm filthy dirty, and you don't even want to see me—"

His heart softened as he imagined the rough two days she must have had. Cowboy work was hard enough on a man, let alone a woman who had only lately done any work at all. Did she have any idea how endearing he found her at this moment? Of course he was glad to see her. Too glad.

"Now, now." He patted her shoulder awkwardly, not wanting to risk an embrace. She had no such compunctions. Her arms went around him, and she cried into his chest. Only the fact that she was as dirty as he was kept him from pushing her away. He rubbed her back and smoothed her snarled hair, which was half up and half down. Slowly the sobs dwindled to sniffles.

He grew very aware of her arms around his waist, of her head against his chest, of her womanly shape beneath the manly clothes. A fire burned in him, and he fought it with all his might. He drew back, placing his hands on her shoulders. Her tears had run down her face, leaving clean rivulets against her dirty cheeks.

She looked at him with all the love in her heart, and his heart nearly burst in his chest. His legs, weary from the day's work, went weak and shaky. Did she know what she did to him?

His forehead fell against hers, his eyes closing. *Dear God, how much can a man bear?* He felt her breath against his lips and shuddered. He was aware of her hands, still at his waist. She was here. With him. No one else was around. His nose brushed hers. Once. Twice. He was almost dizzy with wanting her. Just a kiss. What would it hurt?

His lips were a whisper away when he felt it. That kick in the gut from his soul, knowing that what he was about to do was wrong. A groan ripped from his mouth as he tore away.

He turned and walked a few paces away. Still his heart rioted, and his chest heaved. It was sweet agony. "We can't. It's wrong," he whispered, knowing she couldn't hear.

"I love you." The words were a plea that wounded his heart and brought unspeakable joy at the same time. *Why does it have to be this way, God?*

"Let me stay."

"I can't."

"Why are you doing this?"

He turned then. "It's the right thing to do."

"How can you say that?" A tear trickled down, making another path.

He inhaled, filling his lungs, feeling the strain of his chest as it stretched. The breath came out audibly. He saw the ruckus of work beyond her. He needed to get back to it. He needed to get away from her before he did something foolish.

"I want you to go and get cleaned up by the creek. Do you have anything decent to put on?"

She shook her head. "Just another pair of trousers and a shirt."

"That'll have to do."

"I can't change with—how am I supposed to—"

"I'll send Duncan to stand watch. I trust him." The man was too old to be on a roundup anyway. He would send him to escort Mara home in the morning. Until then he had to make sure the other men kept their distance.

He picked up his hat and shoved it on his head. "Let's go get your things."

She followed him through the prairie grass back to the group. After she gathered her clothes, he sent Duncan off with her, asking him to stand guard. Patting the peacemaker at his side, the older man nodded.

All the while she was gone, Clay kept an eye out for any of the men who might wander off to find her. Only when she reappeared and settled by the chuck wagon did he finally relax.

ã

Mara looked across the campfire, where Clay was having a word with one of the other foremen. He'd promised to have a talk with her once the other men got settled into the night's diversions, but Mara was not looking forward to it. He was only going to tell her she would be leaving in the morning.

She shifted on the log, appreciating the clean clothes more than she'd ever appreciated her finest gowns. How good it felt to be clean once again, to have her hair flowing over her shoulders instead of being matted to her head.

The cowboys had given her a wide path all evening. Some of them were sweet, in a bumbling sort of way, but others had intimidated her with their bold stares. She realized she had been naive in thinking she could travel with the group for two weeks. She was grateful Clay had arranged for her to sleep in the chuck wagon tonight.

Mara didn't know Clay had approached until he was between her and the fire. "We need to talk."

Mara stood, looking at his silhouetted form and wondering what expression he wore. She followed him a short way to the chuck wagon. Far enough away not to be heard, close enough to avoid speculation.

He leaned against the back of the rig. She could see his eyes now, though they were shadowed by the wagon. She thought of their embrace hours before and wished he would take her in his arms again. Instead he folded them across his chest.

A lively harmonica tune started in the distance, and she could hear the sizzling and popping of the fire from where she stood. Her body tensed with expectation. She knew she wouldn't like what he was about to say.

"I've asked Duncan to escort you home tomorrow."

She looked into his eyes but couldn't figure out what he was thinking. He held his body rigid. His face was a mask of indifference. She knew she couldn't stay. It wasn't practical or even safe. She had hoped he might escort her home, though she knew it would be inappropriate.

"I trust him to see you safely home. If you make good time, you'll be home by nightfall."

Home. She would have to tell her parents where she'd been. She shouldn't have lied to begin with. *Lord, I've failed You again. Will I ever learn?*

"Say something." His voice was scratchy, like the stubble that covered his jaw.

"I don't want to leave you."

Shadows played over his face as his jaw clenched. "This isn't about what we want. It's about what's right."

How many times would they go over this? How could he deny her what she most wanted?

"Your parents aren't believers."

His words confused her. What bearing did that have in all this? He must've read her thoughts.

"The Bible is clear on a child's duty toward her parents."

She opened her mouth. "But I'm—"

He held up his hand. "I know you're no longer a child. I'm all too aware of that fact." He gave a wry grin.

Heat kindled in her at his admission. A small part of her was glad it pained him too. She wondered if that was selfish.

"You're new to the Christian faith. But what kind of example would it be for us to defy your parents?"

She hadn't thought of that. And she did want desperately for her parents to find what she had found. So far they wouldn't even go to church with her. Her mother's words haunted her. *"I'll not sit in the same building with that heathen."* The words brought an ache to her heart even now as it had then.

He reached into his pocket and pulled out a small book. He handed it to her, and she saw it was a Bible. Its edges were curled, the pages frayed.

"I want you to have this."

She realized it was his. "I can't take your Bible, Clay."

She handed it back, but he refused to take it. "I marked some passages earlier tonight. Read them. It'll help you understand why I'm doing this, because, believe me, Mara, this isn't easy for me either."

Her hand fell to her side. She read the pain on his face and knew he suffered too. "I'll read them."

He nodded once then started to walk away. She watched him every step of the way.

When he turned back, her heart lurched. "Duncan will settle down in front of the wagon, and I'll bed down behind it."

She nodded, unable to speak around the knot in her throat. She climbed into the chuck wagon and laid down on the spot they had cleared for her. It wasn't her safety she worried about; Clay would protect her. But who would protect her heart from the pain of losing him?

twenty-one

The ride back to Cedar Springs the next day was long and tedious. The weather had grown noticeably cooler, and Mara was grateful for it. She had many hours to think back on her last morning with Clay. Not that there was much to think about. He had rushed through breakfast and hurried to get saddled up like the rest of them. He had barely spoken two words to her, but she knew in her heart that he ached as she did.

Duncan led them at a gallop, and her backside was in no shape for the beating. No wonder ranchers stayed so trim and brawny. Duncan had been a gentleman through and through, she had to admit, even if he did set a difficult pace.

By the time they reached town, dusk was setting in, and Mara dreaded the confrontation with her parents. She knew now she must tell them the truth. Clay had been right. She had to show them Christ's love with her obedience if she ever hoped to reach them.

She wished she could change into proper attire before seeing her mother, but it was the dinner hour, and her family would undoubtedly be seated around the table. She would have no way of sneaking to her room first. She sighed deeply as the horse drew to a halt. She was ever so glad to dismount. When she did, her muscles ached as she stood straight.

"You be all right now, Miss Lawton?"

She nodded. "Thank you for seeing me home safely."

"Glad to oblige." Duncan touched the brim of his hat and rode away, the hooves of his horse stirring up the packed dirt.

She turned toward her home. Light spilled from the windows, filtered by fine lace curtains. Dread curdled in her stomach. She had wronged her parents, and now she had to face them with it. Why, oh, why did she do such foolish things?

She walked up the porch steps, her weary legs trembling beneath her. How she longed for a hot bath and her feather bed! The door opened easily, and the odor of burning food caught in her lungs. *Some things will never change,* she thought, remembering her own failed efforts with a cookstove.

"Who's there?" Her father's voice boomed from the kitchen, followed by the scraping of his chair.

"It's me."

"Mara?" Her mother called, and Mara heard their footsteps. "Why, what are you doing home so—"

They rounded the corner just then, and her mother's words cut off. Her eyes widened, her chin dropped, and her painted eyebrows snapped together. "Why are you dressed like—like a man?"

She opened her mouth to respond.

"Mara, what is the meaning of this?" her father asked.

William joined them then, and Mara knew he had come to see what the excitement was about. She had a childish urge to stick out her tongue. He laughed at the sight of her.

"Get out!" her mother and father said to William at once, her father pointing back toward the dining room for emphasis.

Seeing her mother's face, Mara knew she would not be let off easily. Nonetheless she wanted to get it out of the way. "Mother, Daddy, I know I was supposed to visit Sadie, but that isn't where I went."

Her mother sucked in a breath.

Her father's eyes narrowed.

"This has something to do with that—that—Clay Stedman!" Her mother spat his name as if it were spoiled meat.

"Now, Letitia, don't get all excited."

Mara watched the emotions play on her mother's face. Her hands covered her mouth. "It's true, isn't it?" It was no question. "Oh, my baby girl! You are ruined. Ruined! Who will have you now, I ask? No one, that's who! Word will get around before tomorrow passes, and your reputation will be beyond repair!"

"Come now, Dear—let's let Mara speak for herself," her father said.

They both stared at her. Her father with a this-better-be-good expression, her mother with a horrified one. Had it not been so serious, it would have been comical.

She addressed her mother, who seemed most in need of explanation. "While it's true that I did go to see Clay—"

"Oh, I knew it!"

"Hush, Letitia—let her speak."

"I went on the roundup with the local ranchers." She gestured to her clothing. "That's why I'm dressed like this." She felt her cheeks grow warm. Dozens of men had seen her this way, and she wasn't proud of it.

Nor was her mother. The woman swayed, and her hands suddenly produced a fan that began fluttering in front of her face. "Oh my—"

"Let me get this straight," her father said. "You pretended to be a man—a boy—the entire time?"

She nodded. "It was only yesterday that I was found out."

"What did he do to you, Darling?" Her mother pressed a handkerchief to her eyes.

Mara's stomach churned with anger. Would her mother never learn? Why did she always see Clay through the veil of her prejudices? "He protected me, Mother. That's what he did."

"All those men—" her mother moaned.

"It was foolish of me, I admit. But nothing happened. Clay insisted on sending me home—"

"As well he should!" her father exclaimed with a frown.

Mara didn't know if her mother was going to faint or yell. She seemed to waver between the two.

"I shouldn't have gone, and I shouldn't have deceived you. Clay made me see that. I'm deeply sorry, Mother, Daddy." She beseeched them both with her eyes.

Her father softened first, nodding. "Well, there's no harm done, I suppose."

"No harm?" her mother asked. "Why, she's been alone at

night—mind you, at night—with dozens of wretched cowboys, and there's no telling what—"

"Enough, Letitia! We'll leave well enough alone."

Mara looked from one parent to the other. Her father rarely
had the upper hand with her mother, but it looked as if the
woman was backing down. Mara scarcely dared to breathe.

Her mother snapped her mouth shut, and her lips tightened
in a thin line.

"William!" her father called to the next room. "Go and
draw your sister a bath."

Mara sighed as her mother walked away, her back stiff and
unyielding. Her mother probably thought she was not sorry at
all, that she was only manipulating them as she had done in
the past. Mara couldn't blame her. But she would prove to her
parents God had changed her—even if it killed her. And considering the pain constricting Mara's heart, it just might.

❧

After resting from her adventure, Mara remembered the small
black Bible Clay had given her. She retrieved it from her
bureau where she had put it after unpacking. It looked like a
worn, familiar friend. She felt some guilt at taking his Bible.
Did he have another one to read? She should give it back
when she saw him again.

*"I marked some passages earlier tonight. Read them. It'll
help you understand why I'm doing this."*

At the memory of his words she thumbed through the Bible.
The pages parted at the twentieth chapter of Exodus. She
smiled when she saw it was marked with a leaf, a dark, glossy
bittersweet leaf. Verse twelve was underlined.

"Honor thy father and thy mother: that thy days may be
long upon the land which the LORD thy God giveth thee."

She reread the sentence. Did this mean those that honored
their parents lived a longer life? The thought jarred her
and comforted her at the same time. She knew so little about
God and His ways. She was like a newborn in her faith compared to Clay.

She flipped through the pages, and again they fell open, a leaf marking a spot in Colossians chapter three.

"Children, obey your parents in all things: for this is well-pleasing unto the Lord."

He had been right. She shouldn't have doubted it for a minute. He was doing the right thing, much as she disliked what that meant. She picked up the leaf and twirled it between her fingers. She hoped it was not all for naught. She hoped her parents saw that her life was no longer a strangling vine, but a useful thing of beauty.

Other passages were marked.

"If ye love me, keep my commandments."

"Let your light so shine before men, that they may see your good works, and glorify your Father which is in heaven."

"Set your affection on things above, not on things on the earth."

The words she read convicted her, convincing her she needed time to study God's Word. How could she be a light to her parents if she didn't know what was required of her? She promised herself and God right then. She would learn His ways, and she would do her best to live the life Christ called her to, and someday she hoped her parents would trust Him as well.

twenty-two

Autumn's chilly fingers plucked away the colorful leaves of the trees one by one, sending them scuttling across the ground and into piles. Each week fewer and fewer leaves hung from branches until the smell of winter drifted in the brisk breeze.

Mara saw Clay only at church each week, and though she'd tried to return his Bible, he had shaken his head and showed her he had another. It was hard seeing him every Sunday. When their eyes would meet, they would exchange sad smiles and go on their way. Beth was the only bright note in her days and her only source of information about Clay. She couldn't keep from asking after him whenever Beth would come to visit.

Mara was almost relieved when the frigid days of winter moved in, bringing with it drifts of snow and sparkling icicles. People holed up in their snug homes, daring to go out only when necessary.

Church was often cancelled in the winter when snow lay thickly on the ground. Many church members lived too far to risk exposure during the coldest months, and few had sleighs for transportation.

Mara busied herself with sewing and chores. She even taught her mother some basic stitches. She made shirts for her father and William for Christmas and an apron and scarf for her mother. Beth showed up a few days before the holiday with a pair of mittens she had knitted. Mara gave her the doll she had sewn, complete with a tiny dress and bloomers.

She had wanted to make something for Clay. Oh, how she'd wanted to. But doing so would only worsen the pain for them both. She knew she was right when, as Beth left that afternoon, she passed on words from Clay.

"Tell Mara I said Merry Christmas and that I'm thinking of her."

Her stomach knotted at the words. *Oh, Clay, I'm thinking of you too—every minute of every day.* But she hadn't said the words to Beth. She couldn't say anything for the lump in her throat. She only nodded.

She often found her mother looking at her oddly while they cooked or did laundry together. Though she hadn't said anything, Mara thought she must be confused about the changes in her daughter's life. Once her mother had walked by her bedroom when she was teary-eyed over Clay. Her mother had asked if something was amiss, but Mara said she was fine.

She read the Bible in the parlor in the mornings, and once her father asked where she'd gotten it. Across the room her mother stiffened when she told him Clay had given it to her, but she said nothing.

When an accumulation of snow melted away in mid-February, Mara both looked forward to and dreaded returning to church. How she longed to see Clay again, but she knew it would be agony as well. She prayed repeatedly for God to take away the feelings if they weren't pleasing to Him, but thus far He had done anything but.

One afternoon, as she and her mother peeled potatoes for supper, her mother surprised her. Mara had been thinking of Clay, wondering what he was doing, how he and Beth were getting along, when her mother spoke suddenly.

"You love him, don't you?"

The shock of hearing the words erased any response from her mind. Her mother continued to peel the potato, but her lips stretched in a taut line. Still, Mara had to be honest.

"Yes."

Her stomach flipped uneasily, and her fingers seemed clumsy in her attempts with the paring knife. She expected her mother to be furious or disgusted by her admission. But if she was, she remained silent. Though the lack of response unsettled Mara, she realized later that it was a good thing.

Perhaps her mother was beginning to see the truth. Perhaps she would see Mara's obedience and Clay's honor and change her mind about him.

No, she refused to let herself think that. It would be unbearable to let herself hope and be disappointed all over again.

Yet, on Sunday, when her mother arrived at the breakfast table wearing one of her nicer dresses, Mara was astonished.

"You needn't stare, Mara," her mother said. "I have been to church before, you know."

Mara wasn't about to point out that it had been years. She was too delighted to say anything for fear her mother would change her mind. Though her father and William stayed home, she was thrilled at what she hoped was God working in her mother's heart.

At church she had the pleasure of seeing the shock on Clay's face when he saw her mother at her side. His sad smile changed as his mouth curved up at the corners. When her mother turned to greet the pastor's wife, he winked at Mara. Oh, how her heart fluttered. Her knees turned weak, and she felt empty inside with wanting him.

His gaze did not meet hers again that day, but she relived that wink at the end of every night when her eyes closed and her body relaxed against the feather mattress.

God was teaching her so much through her separation from Clay. She was learning to depend on Him and Him alone. She was learning how to treat others and how to ask forgiveness for past offenses. She was learning that her worth was not in what she had or of whom she was born. It was in the fact that God had made her, that God had sent His Son to die for her.

The lessons were harder than anything she had ever learned. But Sara reminded her frequently that God never said it would be easy—only that He would be with her through it. And He was. Mara could feel His presence.

Hope surged in her when her mother began attending church every Sunday the weather allowed. She even began asking Mara questions. She didn't know the answers to some of them, but she searched her Bible each day to find answers for her mother. She prayed heartily that God would draw her father and brother to Himself also but took heart that her mother seemed to be coming around.

One week in March, after the last snowfall had melted away, leaving slushy puddles, a period of rain began pelting the winter-frozen ground. Elk River, to the north of town, began swelling with the melted snow and spring torrent. Though the banks were usually high enough to sustain a substantial amount of rain, the hardened ground refused to absorb the extra water, and the people of Cedar Springs began to worry that the waters would come rushing through the town streets.

When the second week brought no respite from the rain, the bells of the church rang one morning announcing an emergency town meeting. At her father's instructions Mara stayed home with her mother and began packing while her father and William went to the church house. It had reached the point where the town needed to be evacuated to ensure safety. Though the Lawtons' house sat on a rise, they thought it prudent to stay elsewhere.

Mara packed her things first and then went to the kitchen to pack some food since they would have to move to someone else's home until it was safe to return. By the time she'd finished packing the food, her mother was still putting together her own things.

Moments later Mara heard a noise outside. Peering out a window, she saw her father and William sloshing through the puddles while wagons drove by briskly on their way to their homes.

"Mother!" she called up the stairs. "Are you almost finished? The meeting's over. We need to hurry." She gathered the bags by the door so her father could load them.

The door burst open, and her father and William barged through, water dripping from their hats.

"Where's your mother?" her father asked.

"She's upstairs still. What's happening?"

"Will, get the wagon hitched." Her father started up the stairs. "Letitia, we need to leave right away!"

"I haven't finished," Mara heard her call. "I need to pack a few more gowns."

"You'll have to leave them." His voice faded, but Mara could still hear him. "We'll be going to the Dearborns', but we must leave now! The river is about to crest. Hurry!"

Mara picked up two satchels in each hand and opened the door. She could load the wagon while Will hitched the horses. She dashed across the ground while rain beat at her head and clothing.

She didn't see the wagon that had pulled up beside her until Clay stepped in front of her. He took the satchels from her hands. "I'll load these. Where are your parents and brother?" He had to shout over the pouring rain.

"Will's hitching the team. Mother and Daddy are inside getting the other things."

"There's no time. The water could crest anytime! We'll take mine." He threw the satchels into his own wagon and raced toward their house.

"Will!" She had to shout his name again before he heard. "Leave the wagon. There's no time!" She gestured toward Clay's wagon, and he seemed to understand.

Mara followed Clay to the house. His long legs had covered the ground quickly, and she hurried behind him, her heart pounding painfully in her chest. For the first time, fear balled up in her stomach. What if they didn't make it out in time? The town lay in a valley beside the river. If the water crested, it would send a raging flood through the streets of Cedar Springs.

Father in heaven, keep us safe!

When she entered the house, her parents were coming down the steps laden with boxes and valises. Clay took her mother's burden. "We'll have to hurry. We don't have much time."

He ushered the group to his wagon. In their haste her parents didn't seem surprised or disgruntled to have Clay there. In fact, they seemed relieved for the help. The rain pummeled them until it had drenched them, running into their eyes, clinging to their hair.

They threw the bags into the back. Clay lifted Mara into the wagon as her father helped her mother onto the seat. Her father and Will had no more settled beside her than they felt, more than heard, the rumbling ground. They looked at one another with widening eyes. Terror snatched the breath from Mara as she turned and saw a wall of water raging past the church and toward them at an alarming rate of speed.

twenty-three

Screams echoed over the roar of water. And above the shrieks Mara heard Clay's frantic call, "Hold on!"

She grabbed the side of the wagon, but the water hit with a force that knocked her from it. Cold water clutched her body and flung her along its violent path. She went under, her heavy dress pulling at her. Water flooded her mouth, and terror filled her stomach.

Help me, God! The raging waters dragged her swiftly. She flailed her arms and kicked her feet. She surfaced, gasping for breath, and saw nothing, her vision blurred by the water. One breath later, she was tugged under again.

She held her breath, fighting the water. It knocked her hither and yon. Her lungs began to burn. She needed air. Desperation surged within her. *Oh, God, help me!*

Her body crashed into something solid. Her head spun with the impact. The force of it knocked the breath from her, and she drew in a lung full of water. She was choking! She fought the urge to breathe in, but her lungs were coughing up the water she'd taken in.

The water pinned her against the object, impeding her progress. In panic she reached out and grabbed on. Its surface was rough, round. A tree. She wrapped her arms and legs around it.

Her insides felt as if they would burst. Burning, searing pain filled her lungs. They continued to try to expel the water and, in doing so, brought more in.

She forced her arms and legs to move. Slowly she shimmied up the tree. When her face cleared the water, she stopped and gasped. A wave of water rushed over her again and knocked her head against the trunk. She crawled up the tree until her head cleared the water.

She drank in the air, coughing and choking. The force of water trapped her against the tree. When she could breathe again, she looked around. *Clay! Mother, Father, Will!* She longed to cry out for them but had no breath to do so. Her eyes scanned the watery grave around her. She saw no one. Her mother's wooden hairbrush floated by. The water had carried her through town and down the road that now served as a ditch for the flow. Hills rose on either side of the water, and she saw that she was within a few feet of safety.

Then, coming toward her, her mother burst to the surface, her arms waving frantically. "Mother!" Mara called, but the woman went under again as she passed by.

Desperate to save her mother, she loosened her grip around the tree.

"No!" she heard, and her eyes scanned the distance. Clay! "Hold on! I'm coming!"

He ran toward her, his feet flying over the ground like a stallion's. She looked downstream and saw her mother surface again. *Help her, Lord! Help us all!*

When Clay reached her side, he knelt down and extended his arm. "Grab on!"

She let go of the tree and reached out. His hand was still inches away. "I can't!" When she leaned toward the bank, the water pushed at her as if trying to tear her from the tree.

Clay grabbed onto a nearby tree with one hand and extended the other to her again. "Reach!"

She tried again, but their fingers were still inches apart. She extended her arm as far as she could, leaning toward the bank, but they were too far away.

"Let go with your arms! Wrap your legs around the tree and reach for me!"

Her legs were already wrapped around the trunk. To let go with her arms made her vulnerable. The water could grab her upper body and carry her away. She looked at Clay then. His eyes shone with fervency, with love.

She let go and reached with her whole body. He grasped

her hand and pulled. She unwrapped her legs, and he pulled her toward shore. He had her in both hands now, and her feet dragged downstream, her dress weighing her down.

She kicked, fighting the water, and Clay pulled her onto dry ground. She collapsed beside him in a heap. "My mother!" She pointed downstream.

"Are you all right?" He held her shoulders.

She nodded, breathless.

"I'm going after her." With that, he turned and ran.

Mara pulled herself up. He might need her help. She stumbled along behind him. The distance between them lengthened as he ran on ahead. She walked and ran for a long time, her sodden dress clinging to her legs. She scanned the water. It was moving faster than she, and she realized she would never catch up with her mother at this rate. Only Clay could save her.

Dear God, help my mother! She doesn't know You, and I can't stand the thought of her dying now!

Her skirts tangled around her legs, and she nearly stumbled and fell but caught her footing and trudged on. Had her mother gone under the water for the final time? The woman had not swum since she was a young girl, and the raging current was dangerous for even the most proficient swimmer. She watched the water as she ran. Limbs and branches tossed about in the waves.

She saw Clay ahead in the distance. He was still running alongside the water, and Mara's heart sank as she realized he hadn't spotted her mother either.

Then, as Mara rounded a slight bend, she tripped over an exposed root and fell face down. The air was driven from her lungs. In that quiet moment she heard it. A faint moaning sound. She crawled to the edge of the drop-off and saw her mother. The woman grasped onto a branch that had caught between the trunks of two trees. She was about fifteen feet from shore, and the force of the water looked as if it would dislodge the branch at any moment.

"Mother, hold on!"

The older woman cried, her panicked gaze meeting her daughter's.

Mara looked around for a branch to reach with, but she found nothing. She looked downstream where she could see Clay scanning the water.

She cupped her hands over her mouth, not knowing if he would hear her over the roar of the water. "Clay!" she shouted. When he didn't respond, she shouted again.

He turned, and she waved both arms. He ran toward her.

"Hang on, Mother! Clay is coming." But as she watched the water tug at the branch her mother clung to, she wondered if he would make it in time. She tried to reach the first tree, a few feet out into the water, but her arm was not long enough. If she stepped into the water, it would surely carry her away too.

Her mother's white fingers held on with determination, but her body had been pulled past the branch. The weight of her and the force of the water would break the branch free of the tangle at any minute. Already the limbs bowed under the strain.

"Hurry, Clay!"

Her mother's eyes were tormented, and Mara knew she was losing hope. "Hold on, Mother! Clay is coming!"

He arrived at her side just then and saw the predicament her mother was in. Immediately his eyes scanned the area, and Mara knew he was searching for a long branch.

"There's nothing. I've already looked! I'll stay with her while you find something!"

"There's no time!"

She saw the branch her mother clutched was bowing and within inches of breaking or becoming untangled from the trees.

Clay jumped into the water before Mara could stop him.

"No!" she shouted. Her stomach grew sick as she watched helplessly.

He dove for the first tree and wrapped his arms around it. The water pulled at his body, but his strong arms held tight to the tree. Two other trees stood between him and her mother.

She watched with horror while he let go of the tree with one hand and grabbed onto the next. Quickly he transferred his other hand to the same tree.

One tree to go. *Please, God, let him reach her in time!* She stood helplessly by.

The next tree was merely a sapling, and Mara wondered if it had the strength to hold him. Her gaze traveled to her mother. The branch was bowing between the two trees and looked as if it would snap at any moment.

"Hurry, Clay!"

He made it to the final tree, though its top bent at his weight. He reached out to her mother.

"Grab on!" she heard him yell to her mother.

She saw the terror in her mother's eyes. She seemed unable to let go. Just then the branch snapped. Her mother's shriek filled the air.

"NO!" Mara yelled.

Clay reached out and grabbed her mother's dress at the shoulder. Her mother found his arm and grasped it for the lifeline that it was. His face strained with the force of the water. He pulled, and the sapling bent under the added weight. When he'd pulled her mother close to him, he yelled, "Grab on!" and her mother reached for the little tree. At the same time Clay reached for the bigger one beside it, still holding on to her mother's arm.

Mara could see Clay's feet kicking, and she knew he was trying to wrap his feet around the tree so that his hands would be free to help her mother.

Mara's breath seized in her lungs. Her whole body shook with fear. Her mother, eyes wild with frenzy, now clung to the sapling with all her might.

Clay reached out for her mother. "Grab onto me!"

Her mother wailed and showed no signs of letting go.

Mara feared that the little tree would break. It was bowing toward the water already like a bulb-heavy tulip. She covered her mouth with her hands. *Let go, Mother!*

"You have to come this way!" Clay yelled. "The tree's going to snap!"

Her mother seemed to register the words and reached out to him, clawing at his arm. Clay clasped her forearm with his hand and pulled her toward him. Mrs. Lawton hugged the tree, her face up against the bark. She coughed and sputtered water.

While she rested a moment, Clay moved to the next tree then coaxed the woman into his arms once again.

One more tree until they were near shore. The water rushed by violently, and Mara knew her mother could slip free of Clay's grasp at any moment. Her arms must be dreadfully tired.

They maneuvered to the next tree, and Mara was relieved she could finally help. She knelt on the shore, grabbing a nearby tree for stability, and reached out her hand while Clay held her mother around the waist. Mara worried she wouldn't be able to hold on, but when her mother's hand clasped hers, she was determined she would not let go.

Mara pulled her mother while Clay pushed from behind. The force of the water was staggering. For a moment she thought they were not making any headway, but a sudden shove from Clay sent her mother toward the shore. Mara pulled, and her mother clambered onto dry land in a sodden heap.

Clay was several feet from safety, and Mara looked into his eyes. She saw determination there, but she wondered if he could span the gap of water between the tree and the shore. Grasping a tree with one hand, Mara extended her other to him.

He reached out and clasped hers and, in a sudden dive, pushed away from the tree and landed with his upper body on shore. Mara let go of his hand and pulled at his shoulders while he kicked his feet and scrambled onto dry ground.

Beside her, her mother coughed and choked up water until she vomited.

With her mother and Clay out of danger, her thoughts turned toward her brother and father. She looked at Clay. "We have to go find Will and Daddy!"

Clay shook his head, catching his breath. "They're all right." He lay on his back gasping for breath, his chest expanding with each shallow breath. "They're back by the bridge. Your father was knocked out. Will stayed with him."

Relief flooded through her. It wasn't until that moment that she realized how exhausted she was. Beside her, Mrs. Lawton lay face down still coughing. Mara patted her back. "You're all right, Mother. Thanks be to God, you're all right."

Her mother whimpered.

Clay sat up beside her. "You're not hurt, are you?" he asked her mother.

The woman shook her head.

Mara felt Clay's hand on her shoulder, and she turned to meet his gaze. His hair lay plastered to his head. Drops of water still clung to his lashes and coursed down his face. Still, he'd never looked better. His gray eyes reflected the pool of water they'd just been saved from.

"Are you all right?" he asked.

She nodded, her eyes tearing up. Thank God that Clay had come along when he had. She put her hand on his. "Thank you."

He squeezed her hand then rose to his feet. "I'll go check on your father. When your mother has recovered, meet us at the Farnsworths'. That's where Doc is staying, and your father will need to be looked over."

Before she could nod, he took off, running through the high grass.

Mara turned back to her mother whose breaths still came in shallow pants. The coughing had subsided somewhat, but her face was pasty white. Mara rubbed her shoulder. "Rest up, Mother. Everything is going to be fine."

❧

Within two days Mara and her family were able to get their home mopped up and dried out. They were fortunate that the floodwaters had not risen much past their front door. Other homes and businesses in the town had sustained more damage.

The Lawtons had spent the first night with the Farnsworths,

so Doc Hathaway could keep an eye on Mara's father. But after some sutures and rest he was fine. Her mother seemed to have changed after the scary experience. She hadn't once mentioned that her favorite gowns had washed away in the flood or that her beautiful imported furniture sported water marks around the legs. As the sun warmed the town with spring-like temperatures, the soil softened, and the floodwaters evaporated.

Mara had not seen Clay in the past week, though she thought of him often. At first, she hoped her mother's change would include a new attitude toward him, but that hope ebbed away with the water. Her mother had mentioned neither Clay nor the way he saved their lives the previous week. Mara couldn't imagine how her mother could still remain prejudiced against the man who'd risked his life to save them.

She pulled up the window sash by her bed to draw in the evening air then sat back down with her sewing. She pulled the needle through the fabric of what would soon be a gown for her mother. She was close to accepting Christ, Mara knew it. Perhaps at church tomorrow. *Let it be so, Lord.*

She had mixed feelings about seeing Clay again. She had relived the flood so many times in the moments before she drifted to sleep. She thought of the intensity in his eyes, the stubbornness in his jawline. Each precious feature was etched in her heart. Would the separation ever get easier? She had thought her feelings might fade with time, but they were getting stronger instead. It seemed so unfair. But then Mara had learned life was anything but fair. And when she thought of Ingrid's death and how Cade and baby Adam were left to finish life alone, she chided herself for complaining.

She had just tied off a knot when she heard her father call up the stairs. "Mara, come down here a minute. There's someone to see you."

She hopped up and set her things aside, wondering if Beth had come to spend the evening with her. She hoped so. Beth always had a way of lifting her spirits.

Mara descended the stairs and entered the parlor where her

parents were prone to sit in the evenings. Her gaze cast a quick glance around the room and stopped when it settled on the lone occupant.

He rose slowly from the settee as if mesmerized by her appearance, his hat clutched in his hands.

"Clay. . ." Any other words were lost in the jumble of emotions within her. Her breath froze, paralyzed with some mixture of shock and elation. She wanted to know the meaning of his presence but hadn't the words to ask.

"Mara." His gaze caressed her, and she could almost feel it tangibly. Chills rose on her flesh, though heat coursed through her blood.

"What are"—she cleared the huskiness from her voice—"what are you doing here?" Where were her parents? It registered that her father had called her downstairs and left her alone with Clay. Hope sprang up in her heart, but she tamped it down so as not to be disappointed.

She couldn't deny the light that shone from Clay's eyes, that beckoned her forward. She went as if pulled by an invisible rope. She stopped just out of reach.

"I came to speak with your parents." His eyes shone with intensity, sparkled with fervor. "I've missed you," he whispered.

Her heart crumbled. She nodded. "Me too."

"I could have lost you last week and would never have known—would never have known the full joy of being loved by you."

Her vision blurred as tears formed.

"I came to ask your parents for permission to court you."

Her heart raced. "What?" She had heard him well enough but was surprised he dared face her mother when they both knew full well—

"I passed your mother in the mercantile this week. She actually said hello." His lips curved at one corner.

She tried to read his face, his eyes. Could it be true? Had her parents given him permission? She felt she would burst if he didn't answer her unspoken question soon.

"They said yes." His voice was filled with wonder, didn't quite believe it himself.

She released her pent-up breath and blinked, releasing tears, clearing her vision. Both hands covered her mouth. She was afraid to believe, but there could be no doubt of his meaning as his eyes smiled down at her.

"Mara Lawton, may I have permission to court you?" His voice was husky. His eyes twinkled.

She nodded vigorously. Elation rose within her as Clay took her in his arms and held her. She rested her face against his chest. His heartbeat echoed her own.

"I can hardly believe it," she said.

She felt Clay's chin rest on her head, heard his words whispered into her hair. "I'd have asked for your hand in marriage, but I didn't want to push my luck."

Laughter bubbled up within Mara. She looked up at Clay and knew her eyes were shining with all the joy in her heart. "I would've said yes," she whispered.

"Keep that in mind for later." A smile touched his lips before he leaned forward and sealed the promise with a kiss.

epilogue

"What God hath joined together, let no man put asunder." Pastor Hill's voice boomed across the church. "Clay, you may kiss your bride."

Mara turned to meet Clay's gaze. An autumn breeze flowed through the window, ruffling his hair. His eyes smiled before his lips, and her heart soared with the newfound joy of being his. When their lips met, a fire kindled in her stomach, and the heat found its way clear to her toes. He was hers at last, and she vowed never to take for granted what God had given them.

As they parted, she heard her mother's sniffles. The woman's emotional displays had punctuated the ceremony, but Mara knew her mother's tears fell because she feared she was losing her baby.

Clay winked at her, and she held back a smile as they began their journey down the aisle. Her mother had accepted Clay's Indian heritage months ago. She'd changed in many ways, but best of all she had committed her heart to Christ earlier in the summer.

The congregation met them at the back of the church, giving hugs and best wishes. Clay kept Mara in the strong curve of his arm through most of the procession, and she bathed in the comfort of his presence. When the last of their friends had left the building, she started to follow, but Clay grabbed her hand and pulled her back into the empty coat cubby.

She smiled, loving the impish look in his eyes as he pulled her near for a private kiss. She melted into his embrace, forgetting for a moment the people waiting beyond the doors with handfuls of rice. She wrapped her arms around him, bouquet and all. His touch was warm and gentle, and she leaned into him, loving him with every part of her.

When she pulled away, it was only so she could meet his gaze. "I love you, Clay Stedman."

Her heart paused at the look on his face. "And I love you, Mara Stedman."

She thrilled at the sound of her new name. She was his, and he was hers. They were joined as one before God and man, and the idea of it delighted her.

For a moment the corners of his lips fell, and his eyes grew serious. "Do you think your mother's going to be all right?"

A knot of concern tightened in her stomach. Did he think her mother didn't want him for a son-in-law? "Oh, Clay, you know Mother doesn't feel that way anymore. They're happy tears."

Clay squeezed her hand, the corner of his lip turning up. "I didn't mean it that way. Maybe I was doubtful when I asked their permission to marry you, but when she started making little baby gowns weeks ago—"

Mara tapped his arm, heat blooming in her cheeks at the thought of carrying Clay's baby one day. "We need to get out there," she said, more to change the topic than anything else. She grasped her bouquet with both hands and started to turn, but he held her back.

"Are those bittersweet blossoms?"

Mara nodded, looking down at her bouquet of purple-blue flowers, pleased that he'd noticed. A few leafy vines hung gracefully from the arrangement. She had chosen the vine as a way of remembering on this special day how her life could be a thing of destruction or a thing of purpose and beauty.

Clay's eyes warmed, and he pulled her close again, the bouquet crushed between them.

From around the corner she heard the door whoosh open, ushering in the chatter from outside. "Yoo-hoo!" Pastor Hill called. "Are a bride and groom in here?" In the background she could hear her mother sobbing hysterically.

She giggled and saw Clay try to stifle a smile. His embrace tightened.

"Clay. . .everyone's waiting."

He kissed the tip of her nose. "All right, my Bittersweet Bride," he said. "I'll share you for awhile, but after that you're all mine."

A Letter To Our Readers

Dear Reader:

In order that we might better contribute to your reading enjoyment, we would appreciate your taking a few minutes to respond to the following questions. We welcome your comments and read each form and letter we receive. When completed, please return to the following:

Rebecca Germany, Fiction Editor
Heartsong Presents
PO Box 719
Uhrichsville, Ohio 44683

1. Did you enjoy reading *Bittersweet Bride* by Denise Hunter?
   ❑ Very much! I would like to see more books
      by this author!
   ❑ Moderately. I would have enjoyed it more if

   _____

   _____

   _____

2. Are you a member of **Heartsong Presents**? Yes ❑ No ❑
   If no, where did you purchase this book?_____

   _____

3. How would you rate, on a scale from 1 (poor) to 5 (superior), the cover design?_____

4. On a scale from 1 (poor) to 10 (superior), please rate the following elements.

   _____ Heroine   _____ Plot

   _____ Hero   _____ Inspirational theme

   _____ Setting   _____ Secondary characters

5. These characters were special because_____

_____

_____

6. How has this book inspired your life?_____

_____

_____

7. What settings would you like to see covered in future **Heartsong Presents** books?_____

_____

_____

8. What are some inspirational themes you would like to see treated in future books?_____

_____

_____

9. Would you be interested in reading other **Heartsong Presents** titles?   Yes ❏   No ❏

10. Please check your age range:
   ❏ Under 18   ❏ 18-24   ❏ 25-34
   ❏ 35-45   ❏ 46-55   ❏ Over 55

Name _____

Occupation _____

Address _____

City _____ State _____ Zip _____

Email _____

Magnolias

Just as a seed must endure the pain of change to bring forth a flower, so must Lily Edwards' family experience transformation.

Drift along with this family as the South's old ways are ushered out to make room for the new. How will God help them hold on to the good of the past while embracing a vastly different future?

Historical, paperback, 496 pages, 5 ³⁄₁₆" x 8"

❤ • ❤ • ❤ • ❤ • ❤ • ❤ • ❤ • ❤ • ❤ • ❤ • ❤ • ❤ • ❤

Please send me _____ copies of *Magnolias*. I am enclosing $5.97 for each. (Please add $2.00 to cover postage and handling per order. OH add 6% tax.)

Send check or money order, no cash or C.O.D.s please.

Name_____

Address _____

City, State, Zip _____

To place a credit card order, call 1-800-847-8270.

Send to: Heartsong Presents Reader Service, PO Box 721, Uhrichsville, OH 44683

❤ • ❤ • ❤ • ❤ • ❤ • ❤ • ❤ • ❤ • ❤ • ❤ • ❤ • ❤ • ❤

Hearts♥ng Presents
Love Stories Are Rated G!

That's for godly, gratifying, and of course, great! If you love a thrilling love story but don't appreciate the sordidness of some popular paperback romances, **Heartsong Presents** is for you. In fact, **Heartsong Presents** is the *only inspirational romance book club* featuring love stories where Christian faith is the primary ingredient in a marriage relationship.

Sign up today to receive your first set of four never-before-published Christian romances. Send no money now; you will receive a bill with the first shipment. You may cancel at any time without obligation, and if you aren't completely satisfied with any selection, you may return the books for an immediate refund!

Imagine. . .four new romances every four weeks—two historical, two contemporary—with men and women like you who long to meet the one God has chosen as the love of their lives. . .all for the low price of $9.97 postpaid.

To join, simply complete the coupon below and mail to the address provided. **Heartsong Presents** romances are rated G for another reason: They'll arrive *Godspeed!*